THANKSGIVING IN HOLLYBROOK

Amish Romance

BRENDA MAXFIELD

Tica House
Publishing

Sweet Romance that Delights and Enchants!

Personal Word from the Author

Dearest Readers,

Thank you so much for choosing one of my books. I am proud to be a part of the team of writers at Tica House Publishing who work joyfully to bring you stories of hope, faith, courage, and love. Your kind words and loving readership are deeply appreciated.

I would like to personally invite you to sign up for updates and to become part of our **Exclusive Reader Club**—it's completely Free to join! We'd love to welcome you!

Much love,

Brenda Maxfield

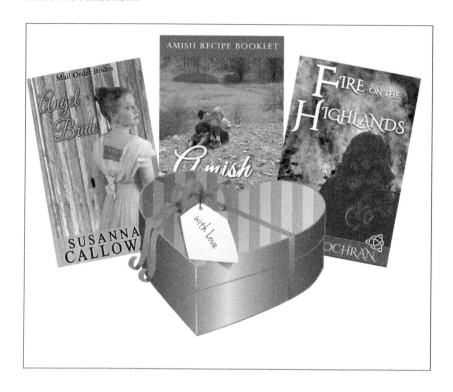

VISIT HERE to Join our Reader's Club and to Receive Tica House Updates:

https://amish.subscribemenow.com/

Chapter One

> Enter into his gates with thanksgiving, and into his courts with praise: be thankful unto him and bless his name.

— PSALMS 100:4 KJV

Leora jolted upright in bed and looked about in confusion for a moment, before her mind cleared. She wiped the sweat from her upper lip.

Again. It had happened *again*.

She threw off the heavy quilt and swung her legs over the bed, getting up quickly, her bare feet padding across the cold floor. She went to the window and pulled the white linen curtain aside, peering out onto the barren yard. The sky was clear, and the moon shone on the frozen ground, sending up sparkles of light.

She blinked and realized she was crying. She squeezed her eyes shut and tried to shake it off.

But it wouldn't shake off. She drew in a long, quivering breath. She still felt her husband's tender touch, still felt his embrace, his kisses. She fancied that she could even smell him—smell his earthy scent mingling with the faint hint of shampoo and soap.

She shuddered.

One year. It had been one entire *year* since she'd lain in his arms. One long, lonely year. So why did it seem like only yesterday? Like only minutes had passed since he...

She put her arms around herself, pressing them against her stomach. After the dreams, she always felt nauseous. She had no idea why—it certainly didn't make any sense. But there it was. She turned from the window and in the narrow stream of light falling across the floor, she made her way back to her bed. She pulled the quilt up to her chin and stayed very still.

Sometimes, after a dream, she could fall back asleep. Other times, sleep wouldn't even tiptoe near her. Without waiting another minute, she knew which it was going to be that night. With a heavy sigh, she got back up and pulled on her robe. She went out to the kitchen and fumbled a bit before getting the lantern lit. The room sprang to life, and she put the kettle on.

Sinking down onto a kitchen chair, she waited in the cold, echoing silence. When the kettle finally whistled, the piercing sound was welcome.

Mostly, Leora was used to living alone. And mostly, she didn't mind it. But right then, at that moment, it was as if she were the only person left on earth. The solitary human woman, eking out her existence alone and unaided...

She made a soft snorting sound. *Don't be ridiculous,* she scolded herself. *You're perfectly fine.*

She poured the hot water into the waiting mug and plopped a chamomile teabag into it. She carried it to the front room and sat in the rocking chair, putting her hands around the almost-too-hot mug to absorb its warmth. She made no move to take a sip. She made no move at all, really. She simply sat there, staring at nothing, until the hot mug turned cold in her hands.

Leora was nearly ready; all she had to do was put on her heavy winter cape and wrap a scarf around her neck. The Jeffreys would be expecting her soon, and she didn't like to be late. Not that she ever was, but still.

She was fetching her woolen scarf from the washroom when she heard the buggy. Her ears pricked. Who would be coming to visit her that early? She hurried back to the front room to peer out the window. Martha—with her two children in tow.

Leora threw open the front door and stepped out onto the porch to greet her best friend. "Martha? *Ach*, but you're a surprise this morning."

"I know, I know," Martha said, climbing out of the buggy holding little Louisa. Ben, being all of four years old, clambered out by himself.

"I was just leaving…"

Martha nodded. "I can see that. Where are you heading?"

"Just some chores," Leora said vaguely, knowing she wasn't fooling Martha for a second.

"Right." Martha walked around the buggy and climbed the steps. "Can't you spare a few minutes? I packed up the *kinner* to come see you. And what with all the boots and coats, that's no small task."

Leora grinned. "Of course. Come in."

They all went inside, and Leora went straight to the heating stove to chuck in another log. Martha peeled off her coat and the children's coats. They shed their boots right inside the door. Martha rarely stayed for only a few minutes, so Leora would be late to the Jeffreys that day, after all.

Martha heaved a great groan and sat down, lowering Louisa to the floor. Leora quickly fetched the box of wooden toys she kept for just such occasions. She dumped them into the middle of the floor, and both children went right to them.

"You were going to your job, *ain't so?*" Martha asked, giving Leora a frank look.

"*Jah.*"

"I don't understand what's so hush-hush about it. You're not the only one in the district who works for the *Englisch*."

"I know. And it's not hush-hush."

"Then why don't you just come out and talk about it like everyone else?"

Why, indeed? But Leora didn't like her entire goings-on laid out before the people. It had been bad enough after David died. Everyone poked their noses into every single detail of her life. What was she going to do now? How would she support herself? ... *What? You mean Leora Fisher is moving off her farm? She's moving to the Yoder's old house? Renting it? That little thing? Goodness, but what is she thinking? Why didn't she just lease her land? It would have given her income...*

But what no one knew—what Leora didn't even know until David's last days—was that their farm was heavily mortgaged. David hadn't paid off anything. In truth, he'd taken out a second mortgage after their first year of dismal crops. So Leora hadn't any choice. She'd had to sell the farm to pay off the mortgages. And even that had barely done it.

So now, she rented. And she had to make that monthly payment, or her next move would be to a loft in someone's barn. She scowled. No. In truth, her next move would have to be to some relative's house in either Linder Creek or Wisconsin—neither of which held any appeal to her at all.

"Leora, you look tired," Martha observed.

"So do you."

Martha burst out laughing. "Of course, I look tired! I have two young *kinner*." She gave Leora a sly look. "And another one on the way. Haven't you noticed my bulging belly?"

Leora's eyes widened. "*Ach!* Are you serious? But that's wonderful *gut* news, Martha."

Martha nodded. "I s'pose it is, but I get tired just thinking about it."

Leora jumped up. "Let me get you some tea."

"I won't say no to that," Martha said. She looked at her two young ones. "Now, Ben, you can share those blocks with Louisa. Come on, now, son."

Ben gave his mother a sour look, but he obediently handed two blocks to his sister, who immediately started beating them on the braided rug. Martha stood and followed Leora to the kitchen.

"Are you going to the youth singing this Sunday after preaching service."

Leora shook her head. "I feel like a fool when I go. I'm much older than most of them, and I've already been married. I don't fit in, Martha."

"You're not the oldest. I happen to know some young men who attend who are older than you."

"Maybe so, but I still don't want to go."

Martha repositioned herself against the counter with a stifled moan. "You need to marry again." She looked around the small kitchen. "You shouldn't be alone like this. It ain't natural."

Leora shrugged. "Natural or not, it's my life."

"I can ask around..." Martha reached out and touched Leora's elbow. "I can see who might be interested in—"

"*Nee*," Leora cut in. "Don't. Please."

"It ain't natural. And you're a fine woman, Leora. You were a *gut* wife to David. You would make a *gut* wife to—"

"*Nee*," Leora cut in again. "Please, Martha."

"You're way too stubborn," Martha observed. "And just so you know, I overheard Deacon Benjamin talking about you."

Leora rolled her eyes. "What now?"

"He was saying it's about time for you to be wed again. And he said that his wife reported to him that you ain't been attending the frolics lately."

Leora faced her. "What frolics?"

"Well, we did have a quilting bee last month, and you didn't come."

"Surely, I wasn't the only woman not there."

Martha shrugged. "Maybe not. But you were the one who's absence was noted."

Leora's jaw tensed. "And just who was the deacon talking to?"

Martha laughed. "Eliza Troyer."

"*Ach!* Eliza Troyer. She's the biggest gossip of all."

"Seeing how she's the owner of the Feed & Supply, it ain't too surprising, is it? She hears everything."

"Wonderful," Leora said, her voice thick with sarcasm. "Now, I s'pose she's talking about my widowhood to everyone who comes into the shop."

Martha chuckled. "I doubt that. I do think it would help if you didn't act so mysterious, though."

"Mysterious?" Leora frowned at her. "I don't act mysterious. That's ridiculous."

"You keep to yourself. It ain't right."

Leora shook her head. "Can we change the subject, please?"

Martha moved to the kitchen table and sank down onto the

bench. "We can. I'm thinking of naming this new one Linda or Peter. What do you think?"

Leora wondered whether she would ever be in the position to name a child. *Her* child. She and David had planned on having children, but in the three years they were married, it hadn't happened. And then, he'd gotten sick and died so quickly, it had left her head spinning. Sometimes, she wished she'd had his child before he died. It would have been a comfort to her. But other times, she wasn't sure. Well, it didn't matter now anyway. It hadn't happened, and that was never going to change.

"I think those two names are right nice," she said to Martha. She busied herself with the cups and teabags, waiting for the water to warm.

"Tom ain't convinced, but he will be," Martha said with a laugh.

There was a howl from the front room, and Martha got up to investigate. Leora finished with the tea and set the steaming cups on the table. Martha returned, shaking her head.

"That Ben is a stinker sometimes, I'll tell you that."

She sat back down and Leora joined her.

"I worry about you, Leora," Martha said, her expression soft.

"You don't need to. I'm fine." But Leora's eyes misted with tears, and she looked down quickly, hoping Martha wouldn't notice. She wasn't used to having someone worry about her, and it felt strangely comforting.

"I know you're fine. You're one of the most capable women I know. But still. You could stop by my house more often. Don't you get lonely?"

Of course, Leora got lonely, but she wasn't about to announce it.

"I'm fine," she repeated. "But I could stop by more, and I will. I promise."

"*Gut*. Because it's getting to be more and more troublesome for me to get out and about. Come spring, it'll be easier. But by then, I'll be as big as a barn."

Leora laughed. "Are you cooking Thanksgiving dinner this year?"

Martha nodded. "Me and my *mamm* and sisters. It'll be at my house. You're coming, *ain't so?*"

Leora nodded. She didn't have any other place to be.

Chapter Two

Leora was a whiz with numbers. It was a bit of a mystery to her, as she'd never put any extra effort into it. But she'd always been able to figure any math problem out—usually in her head without the benefit of paper and pencil. Some women found out about her gift and came to her for help—especially women who had little side businesses.

No men, though. That wouldn't suit.

Which was probably why David had buried the two of them in debt. If he'd only let her help with their finances, she likely could have avoided the mess she'd been left with after he died. But he didn't ask her. The one time she'd offered, his reaction was so swift that she was stunned.

"That's *my* job," he'd told her in no uncertain terms.

"But, David, it's easy for m—"

"Are you implying that it's hard for me? That maybe I ain't as smart as you?"

She'd gaped at him open-mouthed. David was a kind man, not one given to impatience or curt words, so his reaction to her offer was completely unexpected. But it was effective. It shut her up, but quick.

She never offered again.

Nor did she realize the extent of their financial issues until he lay dying in the hospital. The pneumonia had been vicious and fast. The doctors did what they could, but he was too far gone. Leora had sat by his side, in stunned disbelief, as he faded further and further from her grasp.

He struggled to breathe and talk, but he managed to eke out about the second mortgage before he died. He was devastated and ashamed, and she had spent a good while telling him it didn't matter—telling him that nothing mattered except him getting better. But he hadn't gotten better. He'd gotten worse until that awful day before Thanksgiving...

Leora shook off the memories and pushed through the door to Jeffreys Diner. The bell above the door tinkled its welcome. Bill Jeffreys saw her come in from where he stood in the back by the kitchen. He smiled and nodded at her.

He was a handsome man—his thick black hair had a streak of gray near his temple even though he was hardly old enough to have any gray at all. His eyes were dark and deep, and his gaze on her was always intense. Sometimes, he made her shiver, and then she'd wonder why. He was kind and energetic, and his smile was compelling, drawing her in.

His customers loved him, laughing and joking with him whenever he came out from the kitchen onto the floor. And he loved them right back, asking after their children and their jobs. He even remembered the names of their pets.

Leora enjoyed working for him. She appreciated how mesmerized he was by her agility with numbers. He complimented her often, which she wasn't used to, but she reveled in it. Later, of course, when she left the diner after her work, she would scold herself for her vanity, but when his next compliment came, she would eat it up all over again.

Bill worked with his sister, Donna. She was as fair as he was dark, and Leora often marveled that they came from the same parents. Donna worked as the waitress and cashier. During the holidays, they hired extra help, beginning right before Thanksgiving. So, they now had two extra waitresses hired through the middle of January.

Leora arranged their paychecks and hours. She also kept the diner's books. She went in every few days to go over the numbers, check the schedules, and make the orders. At first, she'd balked about doing the ordering. But Bill had talked her into it, saying he and Donna didn't have time, and after all, it was a financial matter and wasn't she in charge of their finances?

Which was true.

Except taxes. Leora had very little knowledge in that arena, so she simply made sure all the books were in order for the tax accountant.

Now, she walked back to where Bill was standing.

"I'm sorry I'm late," she said.

"I was a bit worried is all," he told her, his low voice rich and low.

"I had a visitor that I wasn't expecting."

"Everything's all right, isn't it?"

"*Jah*. It's fine."

"Now, if you had a phone..." he teased.

"I know. I know," she replied, her voice light. "And that isn't going to happen."

He touched her shoulder. "We both know that."

She shrugged. "I'll get busy."

He smiled. "So will I. The orders don't cook themselves."

"*Nee*, they don't."

"I may need to hire a part-time cook over the next few weeks. Do we have the money for it?"

He was teasing again. Even though she kept the books, he knew full well what their bottom line was. He knew where every penny went, so of course, he knew they had the money.

"Hmm." She pretended to consider it. "I'm not sure you do. You may have to simply work harder. Cut back some."

He laughed and went back into the kitchen. She walked to the tiny office located right inside the kitchen. She liked working so close to the cook stoves. The different aromas from all the orders were tantalizing and enjoyable. Sometimes, Bill brought in a sample of something for her to try, and it was always delicious. He was a great cook, as evidenced by his loyal clientele.

Now, she pulled her chair back and sat down. She took the ledgers from the side drawer of the desk and opened them. Bill had been after her to use the computer, but so far, she had resisted. She knew he was accommodating her old-fashioned way of doing things and that no one else in town kept books like she did anymore. She also knew that the day was coming when she'd either have to learn the computer or quit.

She didn't want to quit.

She liked her job, and she needed the money.

But what would the bishop say if he got wind of her learning the computer? There were a few Amish in their district who used computers with their businesses—they'd gotten special permission. But this wasn't her business; it was her job. Would that be the same thing?

She wasn't sure, and for some reason, she was hesitant to find out. But in truth, she knew the reason she kept putting it off. What if the bishop denied her permission? What if he told her to quit and find another job? Then, she'd be forced to obey.

She sighed. Martha was right. Her job had become like a secret, even though it wasn't. She needed to be more forthcoming with the people in her district. She needed to be more open, more communicative.

But the plain truth was—she didn't want to.

Noah King helped load the five sacks of chicken feed into the back of his pony cart. Then, he went back inside the Feed & Supply to pay Eliza Troyer, who ran the cash register. She and her husband owned the store and practically lived there. He wondered when they were ever at their house.

"Did you get it loaded?" Eliza asked him, smoothing her hands down her ample bosom.

"It's all loaded," he said. "Can you add the cost to my account?"

She pulled a large ledger from below the register. "Glad to."

"Thank you, Eliza."

She narrowed her eyes. "You courting anyone, Noah?"

He balked. Eliza was a persistent busy-body, but this question was nervy even for her.

She clucked her tongue. "*Ach,* I know it ain't something we discuss freely, Noah, but if you aren't seeing somebody, I've got a lovely niece in Linder Creek who's courting age."

He was still so stunned, he didn't know how to respond, but he did feel his cheeks go hot.

She laughed. "I see I've embarrassed you. Now listen to me, Noah King. Your *mamm* ain't in these parts, I know. So, she ain't here to see to things..."

See to things? Since when did mothers interfere with the girls their sons were courting?

"...so I don't mind stepping in." Eliza leaned forward. "My niece will be coming soon for an extended visit. Her name's Doris, and she's a lovely girl."

"I-I'm sure she is," Noah said, his face still hot. Truth was, he had no interest in Eliza Troyer's niece—even sight unseen. He was smitten with someone else. Someone lovely and kind and right there in Hollybrook. His heart raced even at the thought of Leora Fisher. Not that she'd given him an ounce of encouragement. In fact, she had no idea how smitten he was.

He needed to do something about that, but in truth, Leora could sometimes be a bit unapproachable.

He put it down to shyness. Maybe. Also, Leora had already suffered plenty in her life—what with her husband dying so young and her not having any kinfolk nearby to help her out or even to keep her company.

Maybe he should stop over at her house later that day. Just to say hello and see how she was doing. The very thought made him sweat. Men didn't just stop by a widow's home without a good excuse, and he hardly had one. His mind spun; what excuse could he come up with?

"Noah?" Eliza asked, and her voice homed in like a drill. "You listening to me?"

He gave a start. "*Jah. Jah,* of course, I'm listening."

"Well, mind my words. She'll be here next week, and I'll be asking you over for supper."

"Uh, that's nice, Eliza. I-I need to be going."

She flicked her hand in a gesture of good-bye. "Just mind my words," she repeated while he beat a hasty retreat.

Once back outside in the frigid air, he pulled up the collar of his coat. Leora often rode her bicycle to wherever she was going. That had to be mighty uncomfortable in this weather. And when there was ice, it would be downright dangerous. Surely, she couldn't ride it in the ice.

And there was his excuse. It was a bit of a stretch, and likely she'd never agree to it, but couldn't he offer to take her around in his buggy whenever she needed to go somewhere? He frowned. No, she'd never agree to it. She'd never agree to being seen in public with him when they weren't a couple.

But he could offer. It would be gentlemanly of him. And it would give him an excuse to stop by that very day. Pleased with himself now, he climbed into his cart and snapped the reins. Flicker immediately got underway, moving into a trot without much encouragement from him.

"*Gut* girl," he called out, his mind busy with the details of his plan.

Chapter Three

Leora was pulling on her mittens, when Bill showed up in the doorway to her office.

"Please tell me you didn't ride your bike in today," he said.

She didn't answer, just smiled.

"Oh man, Leora, it's freezing outside. If you stay a bit longer, I can take you home. I'll throw your bike in the back of my pick-up."

"That's not necessary. I'm almost ready to leave, and I'm well-bundled. No reason to fret."

"Fret?" he repeated. "And why shouldn't I fret? My brilliant bookkeeper is about to embark on a mile or more journey on a bike in the middle of winter weather. I've told you a hundred times, Leora, that we can figure something else out."

She pulled on her second mitten. "Not necessary," she said again.

"I think it is." He stepped closer and tweaked the end of her scarf. "I don't want you getting sick on me, now do I?"

She laughed. "I never get sick."

"Then I don't want you taking a tumble and being laid up."

She shook her head, still laughing. "Don't be silly," she said. "I'm telling you, I'm perfectly fine."

He turned and hollered at his sister. "I need to leave for a while."

Donna scurried over. "How's that possible?" she asked, wiping her hands down her apron. "Who'll cook?"

"Can't you take over the griddle for an hour? The two girls can handle the floor."

Donna gave him a dirty look. "Bill, I can't cook like you."

"Sure, you can," he said. "You've done it before."

"And I didn't like it."

Leora stepped forward. "There's no call for him to leave," she told Donna. "I'll see you in two days."

"I'm taking you home," Bill insisted. He turned to his sister. "Less than an hour, then."

Donna groaned. "Fine. But if you take longer than an hour, I'm closing the diner."

He laughed. "As if you'd do that. Come on, Leora. This won't take long."

Leora didn't follow at first. She didn't want him to take her home. Well, that wasn't exactly true. She did enjoy riding in his truck with him, and she did enjoy his company. But this was silly. She rode her bike in the winter months all the time, and it wasn't slick out today. She'd be fine. Cold, but fine.

"Leora," he said, and her name on his lips was so melodious, so earnest, that she weakened.

"Oh, go on," Donna said grumpily. "You know he won't give up till he has his way. I'll be fine."

"You're sure?"

"I'm sure. Now, hurry up so he can get back."

Still reluctant, she followed Bill out the back door of the restaurant to where his truck was parked.

"You go ahead and get in," he told her. "I'll run around to the front of the diner and grab your bike."

Dutifully, Leora climbed into his truck and secured her seat belt. She sincerely hoped no one would see her riding in his truck. Not that it would have been expressly forbidden, but tongues would wag. And they'd wagged enough as far as she was concerned.

In minutes, she watched him through the back window as he hoisted her bicycle into the bed of the truck. Then he ran around and climbed in, a whoosh of cold air following him inside.

"I'll get the heat on pronto," he said, starting the engine. He rubbed his hands together swiftly. "It's freezing in here."

"It's fine," she said.

"You'd say that if it were twenty below."

She giggled. "*Nee*, I wouldn't."

He put the truck in gear and backed out of the parking spot and into the back alley. From there, he pulled onto the main road.

"So, you heat with wood?"

She nodded. "I have a wonderful *gut* warming stove. And my house is small. Well, you've seen my house from the outside."

"I have. Do you chop the wood yourself?"

"Sometimes. Usually, I have the neighbor boy do it for me."

"Good."

She shook her head and smiled. "Goodness, but you must think me helpless. I'm perfectly capable of chopping wood. In fact, I bet I can chop it better than you can."

He laughed outright at that. "You might be right, at that. But someday, I'll chop your wood for you, and then you can make a true assessment."

Chop her wood for her? Her face warmed. That would be completely inappropriate. What if someone came by and saw an *Englisch* man chopping her wood?

He glanced at her and seemed to sense he'd said something wrong. "Uh, if you'd let me, that is," he added.

She only smiled, not wanting to get into it with him. He was a stubborn man, and she certainly didn't want to ignite his stubbornness regarding chopping her wood.

They passed more than one buggy along the way to her house. When they were nearly there, she noted a pony cart pulling into her drive right ahead of them. Why, it was Noah King. She'd not had much contact with him over the years. She knew him, of course, and thought him to be a nice man, but that was all. What in the world was he doing there?

Filled with curiosity, Leora leaned forward, but then she wanted to scrunch down and hide herself. What would Noah King say to her being brought home by Bill Jeffreys?

Nothing, she thought sternly. *He would say nothing.*

"You have company," Bill said. "Were you expecting someone?"

"*Nee.* It's Noah King. I have no idea what he wants." Why did she feel like she had to justify Noah's presence to Bill? It was none of his business. But that was what she was doing.

"I'll pull in around him," Bill said. "I don't want to spook his horse."

"There's room," she said, appreciating his sensitivity. Too many *Englischers* had no concept of what might spook a horse.

He pulled the truck to a stop at the side of her house. She immediately got out and so did he. He hurriedly took her bike out of the truck bed and rolled it to her porch steps where he leaned it against the railing.

She went over to Noah, who was eyeing Bill.

"Hello, Noah," she said. "What brings you around?"

Before Noah had time to answer, Bill came forward with his hand outstretched. "Hello. I'm Bill Jeffreys. Leora and I work together."

They shook hands, and Leora couldn't help but notice how Noah's gaze intensified.

"*Gut* to meet you," he said.

"Same here. Well, I'll be off," Bill told Leora. "I'll see you in two days, then. And don't be surprised if you get another ride home."

With that, he was back in his truck and pulling out of the

drive. She watched him go, knowing Noah was doing the same. And then she turned back to him.

"Hello again," she said. "What can I do for you?"

Noah seemed flustered. He licked his lips and frowned. Leora waited. This was odd, indeed. He appeared to have no idea why he was there, and she had the distinct impression he was annoyed. But why?

Was he judging her because an *Englischer* had driven her home? Now she was becoming annoyed, too. She drew herself up to her full height.

"Noah? What is it you wanted?" she asked, her voice clipped.

He was clearly trying to decide what to say, and her annoyance faded, replaced once again with curiosity.

"I was, uh, worried," he began, looking around as if seeking someone to help him state his purpose. "It's so cold, and I know you have no buggy."

"It's just as cold in a buggy as on a bike," she said, trying to ease his nervousness now. Of course, what she said wasn't true at all. A buggy was much warmer, particularly if the owner had a propane heater inside.

He gave her a skeptical look. "You know that ain't so, Leora." But he was smiling now, his edginess eased.

"Maybe not, but you needn't worry about me." Goodness, was everyone in Hollybrook worried about her being cold?

"I wanted to offer you my services," he went on. "I am more than glad to take you anywhere you need to go while the weather is so cold."

She stared at him, completely stunned. She could have guessed for a long time and not come up with this as the reason he would stop by.

"That's right kind of you," she said, not wanting to be rude, but certainly unwilling for him to be her personal chauffeur service.

"Just being practical," he muttered as if trying to downplay his offer.

"I will keep that in mind."

"Do you need a ride to the preaching service this Sunday? Or somewhere else before that? Sounds like you're going back to work in two days. Bill Jeffreys indicated as much."

She carefully listened to his tone, trying to discern whether he approved of her working with Bill Jeffreys or not. She didn't hear any censure in his words, which was interesting. That certainly wasn't the case with some of the men in their district.

"He owns Jeffreys Diner, *ain't so?*" Noah continued.

"*Jah.*"

"I've been in there once, but I never saw you."

"I work in the back. With their books."

"With their books?"

"I am an accountant of sorts. Without the official title, of course."

"You do all their ciphering?"

"I do."

He blinked as if digesting this news.

"You thought I was a waitress?"

He nodded sheepishly. "I guess I was wrong."

"I guess you were."

He studied her then, and she felt uncomfortable under his gaze. Now was the moment, she thought. Now was the time when he'd disapprove of her job. But he said nothing, only nodded.

"I s'pose I better be getting along," he told her. "You'll remember, won't you? I'm happy to take you wherever you need to go."

"Thank you, Noah. Like I said, it's right kind of you to offer."

He tilted his head in a gesture of farewell and snapped the reins on his horse's rump. He rolled out of the drive, and Leora went inside, leaning against the back of her closed door.

What was that really about? she wondered. He'd never shown any interest in her before.

Chapter Four

Noah let out a sigh of frustration when he turned onto the main road. That had been a total disaster. He had seen the way she stared at him with unbridled curiosity. She wanted to know why he was suddenly interested in her goings about. And then, the timing. Could it have been more awkward?

That Jeffreys fellow was good-looking. Was Leora smitten with him? The very thought twisted up his throat. The man was *Englisch*. Surely, she wouldn't have fallen for an *Englisch* fellow, would she? No. No. That couldn't be right.

But Jeffreys sure had looked interested in her. Noah had seen the glimmer in his eyes, and he recognized it—for he feared he had the same look in his own eyes. And now that Jeffreys fellow would know of his interest in Leora. Would he step up his game?

Ach, but this wasn't expected.

He'd hoped to go over to Leora's place, offer her a kindness, paving the way for future encounters. He knew Leora's reputation in the district. She was stand-offish, private, not eager to accept help. Since her husband died a year or so ago, she'd sold her farm, moved into that small rental house and begun working in town. No one knew much about what she did, including him.

But working with finances? That was hardly a woman's normal position, was it? Not in their district, it wasn't. Now that he thought about it, though, he did remember some talk years earlier about how good Leora was with numbers. He hadn't paid the information much mind, however. But now, upon remembering, he supposed he shouldn't be surprised at her job.

But did she have to work for the Jeffreys?

Noah pulled the reins slightly to the right, turning down the road toward his own farm. If he was interested in Leora—and he was—he was going to have to be more intent. More focused.

Leora sure had looked pretty, standing there by her porch. Her cheeks had been flushed and her blue eyes had been wide and luminous. He could have stood there for some time, just admiring her, but of course, he would never do that. It would be too forward. Too bold.

But would Bill Jeffreys do it? Gaze at her with obvious admiration? Noah grimaced, a sour taste filling his mouth.

Leora sat at her kitchen table, looking through the window to the barren trees in her front yard. The yard wasn't large, but there were still a good number of trees, and their branches looked forlorn in the bitter weather. The wind was blowing, and the branches rustled slightly—she could almost hear them crackling in the cold. The morning had dawned with such low temperatures, that she dreaded bicycling to the Rabers' barn for preaching service. But if she didn't show up, the tongues would really fly.

So, she'd bundled up and was outside ready to mount her bicycle when Martha and her family pulled in with their buggy.

"Get on in here," Martha called through the window. "You ain't riding that thing in this cold."

Grateful, Leora scurried to do as she was bidden.

"Thank you," she said to both Martha and Tom as she climbed in the back to sit by little Ben. "It is right cold this morning."

"Near to freezing," Martha noted. "We might be in for some snow today."

Leora loved the snow, loved the way it fell to the ground in a soft hush, stilling every sound within miles. There was something achingly beautiful about a new snow coating the world in pure white. But it did cause problems. She had ridden her bicycle in the snow before—once it had been plowed, but it wasn't fun. She feared falling down with every turn of her pedals.

But she wasn't about to express her fear to others.

"You going to the singing tonight?" Martha asked her pointedly.

"We already talked about that earlier last week," Leora reminded her, but it did no good.

"Because if you're going, I can ask someone to pick you up. You certainly aren't going to be riding that bicycle of yours in the dark, and you know it gets dark right early these days."

"I likely won't be going," Leora told her.

"Well." Martha sighed heavily. "We can talk about it more later."

Which she did. After the community meal following the service, Martha had gone on and on about it all the way home. Leora had been grateful when they finally reached her little house.

"Bye," she'd said, climbing out of the buggy as quickly as she could. "Thanks so much, Tom, for the ride."

"Anytime, Leora," he said.

Martha grabbed her hand through the open door. "I can send someone..."

Leora shook her head. "You're as stubborn as an old goat," she teased her friend. "If I change my mind, I promise I won't ride my bicycle."

Martha scowled. "Fine. Come see me this week, all right?"

"All right."

Now, back in her own house, Leora replayed the conversation in her mind, and surprisingly, she was of a mind to attend the singing. If nothing else, it might calm some of the wagging tongues around town. But she'd promised not to ride her bicycle, and even if she hadn't, the prospect of riding in this cold was dismal at best. She could run down to the phone shanty and leave a message for Martha, asking her to arrange for someone to take her after all. But why should Martha have to do that? Wasn't Leora capable of arranging her own ride? Besides, Martha would hardly be standing about outside the phone shanty waiting for her message.

Leora's mind filtered through the possibilities, and she came up with very few people she'd want to bother. In truth, most folks would probably be glad to take her, but she didn't feel comfortable asking them.

Yet, there was Noah King. Hadn't he offered her a ride to wherever she needed to go? He had, but she didn't feel comfortable asking him either. Besides, she had no way to ask him. She didn't know the number of the nearest phone shanty to his place. And even if she did, would he check his messages before the singing started that evening? That would be about as likely as Martha checking hers.

So, the decision was made for her. She wouldn't attend. Next time, she wouldn't be so stubborn, and she'd arrange a ride before leaving the preaching service.

She stood up to pour herself a glass of milk. There was Bill Jeffreys. He would take her. She laughed, her mirth sounding a bit hollow in the empty kitchen. Couldn't she just imagine the reaction if she was delivered to the youth singing in a pick-up truck? She laughed again. It would almost be worth it just to see everyone's expressions.

"*Ach*, you're terrible," she muttered to herself.

But still, it would be funny. And she could call Bill's cell phone from the shanty, and he would answer right away. It would work. She poured the milk into a tall glass and took a sip. No. She would never do that.

She would have a quiet evening at home by herself. Just like she did every evening of her life these days.

Noah put on his woolen coat. He had a heater in his buggy, but he didn't usually turn it on unless the temperatures fell to unbearable lows, and the temperature wasn't that low tonight. He stopped at the door with his hand on the knob.

Would Leora be at the youth singing? He hoped so; although, in truth, he doubted it. She rarely attended. He knew because he'd been watching for her every other Sunday evening for months. So why should she attend that night? And besides, how would she get there?

Maybe he should stop by on his way and see if he could give her a lift. Would she resent his coming? Would it be too forward of him just to stop by to check on her?

The image of Bill Jeffreys's face came to mind. He saw again the look in Jeffreys's eye as he had watched Leora.

No. It wouldn't be too forward.

Now that he decided, he hurried outside to hitch up Flicker. He would turn on his heater. That way, if Leora was home and if she decided to accompany him, the buggy would be toasty warm. With renewed vigor, he hitched Flicker up in record time. He climbed into the buggy and switched on the heater. With a smile on his face, he left his property and headed for Leora's house.

Please say you'll come, he whispered into the warming buggy. *Please say you'll come.*

He pulled up to Leora's porch a short while later. There was light coming from what he assumed was the kitchen, so she was likely home. It wasn't fully dark outside, but the shadows were closing in quickly. He turned on the lights of his buggy and then jumped out to knock on Leora's door.

She pulled the door open and gaped at him in surprise.

"Uh, hello, Leora," he said, hating the nervousness he heard in his voice. "I was on my way to the youth singing, and it occurred to me that you might need a ride." The words rushed from his lips as if the faster he spoke, the better chance he had of her saying yes.

She blinked at him and smiled. "I had thought of going," she admitted.

"Do you have a ride?"

"*Nee*, I don't." She took a step back. "Do you want to come in for a minute while I grab my cape and mittens?"

He grinned. "Sure thing."

He stepped inside, hardly believing his luck. He glanced around the house. It was rather empty, without much furniture, but he still felt a sense of homeyness about the place. He was surprised to see some evergreen branches arranged in a bouquet of sorts sitting on a low coffee table. He'd never seen someone make a display of branches. It was odd, but it had a nice effect. In fact, if he breathed deeply, he could smell the evergreen. It reminded him of Christmas, even though they hadn't yet passed through Thanksgiving.

"I'm ready," she said, emerging from a side door. She was

bundled up in her cape and mittens and a dark burgundy scarf was wrapped around her neck. Her cheeks were flushed as if she'd already been outside in the biting air.

"*Gut*. Shall we go, then?" he asked, walking toward the door.

She followed him outside, and he scurried to the passenger side of the buggy and held open the door for her. She moved past him, climbing inside.

"*Ach*, but it's warm in here," she exclaimed, clearly pleased.

He smiled. "Got the heater installed last winter."

"It feels heavenly," she murmured.

He smiled again, as if he had personally heated the buggy by rubbing two sticks together to make a fire. Telling himself to calm down and take a breath, he shut her door and hurried around to his side. Within minutes, they were underway to the Rabers' barn.

"Do you always attend the youth singings?" she asked him.

"Not always, but often enough," he answered. "You?"

His face went hot. Why had he asked her when he already knew the answer?

"*Nee*, not often," she said, settling back in her seat and gazing out the side window.

He searched his mind for something to say. "Do you have plans for Thanksgiving?" he asked.

She looked at him. "I'll likely go to Martha's house."

He nodded. He knew she and Martha were good friends from way back. "That'll be nice," he said, then cringed. Could he not be a little more interesting?

"*Jah.*" She was quiet for a moment. "And you? Where will you be? You don't have kin nearby either, do you?"

"*Nee*, I don't." In truth, he hadn't been invited anywhere yet. But every year, he would eventually receive an invitation somewhere, albeit sometimes at the last minute.

"I'm sure Martha will have enough for another person..."

"I wasn't fishing for an invite," he said quickly.

"I know you weren't." She fell silent again.

"Some folks go to restaurants for Thanksgiving."

"They do," she said, smiling. "Jeffreys Diner is right busy on Thanksgiving Day. Bill tells me that sometimes, folks have to wait almost a half hour to be seated."

"Is that so?"

"The diner isn't that big, of course. But still, it's packed out on the holidays. Sometimes, folks even go on Christmas Day."

"They're open on Christmas?"

She nodded. "I wondered about that, too, but Bill told me he feels bad for the people who have no place to be. If he keeps the diner open, they come in and it's almost like a big family meal."

Noah found himself getting irritated with all this quoting of what Bill said. "I see."

"Do you go see your relatives at Christmas?" she asked.

"Sometimes. Depends a bit on the weather. If it's really bad, I stay put. If not, I'll hire a driver to take me to Wisconsin."

"Your kin are in Wisconsin? I have family over that way, too."

"Do you?"

She nodded. "But I've never had a hankering to move there. I like Hollybrook."

"So do I." He grinned at her and for a moment, he felt a connection between them, but she quickly looked away.

He turned into the Rabers' drive and added his buggy to the line of buggies already in place.

"Looks like we're late," she observed. "That would be my fault. I'm sorry."

"No need to be sorry," he said. "Being a few minutes late won't hurt anything."

He turned off the lights and the heater and then got out and came around to open her door, but she'd already gotten out.

"I need to see to Flicker," he told her. "I'll be in shortly."

She nodded and walked toward the open barn door.

It wouldn't matter when he wandered inside, for he couldn't sit by her. The males and females sat apart. She likely wouldn't even give him a thought until it was time to go back home. Taking a girl home from the youth singing usually meant that he was courting her. That wouldn't be the case with Leora, although he wished it were. There was something about her that touched him—even when she was being a bit formal with him.

He wished he could hear her laugh. As far as he could tell, she didn't laugh much, but he bet her laugh was amazing. If only he were a bit more amusing, he might be able to get a laugh or two out of her. He wondered if she laughed with Bill Jeffreys.

Stop it, he told himself. *You'll make a fool of yourself if you aren't careful.*

But the image of her laughing with Jeffreys wouldn't leave his mind. It kept popping up during the singing when his mind should have been on the hymns.

Leora had found a spot in the middle of a group of older girls. She looked happy enough to be there. He tried not to stare at her, but nevertheless, his gaze frequently went to the far side of the barn where she was sitting. A lantern hung close to where she sat so he could see her face clearly.

Goodness, but she was beautiful. And when she sang, sometimes she closed her eyes, and he could almost hear her voice rise above the others. She looked positively angelic sitting there. One time, their gazes met and locked for a brief moment. His breath caught and his heart hammered against his ribs. It was a thrilling moment but fleeting as she quickly averted her gaze.

Still. It had happened, and it rocked through him with a sweet deliciousness. He could barely concentrate on the words of the songs after that.

Chapter Five

Leora's cheeks flamed hot. She'd had a suspicion that Noah was watching her. She could feel his gaze. Finally, unable to resist any longer, she'd looked over, and then it had happened. Their gazes met and she felt something zap through her. Instantly sweaty, she'd glanced away as fast as she could. What *was* that?

And why did he keep looking at her? It made her squirm. She was sure the girls around her would notice, but none of them whispered a thing.

She breathed a sigh of relief when the singing portion was over and the refreshments and visiting time began. Everyone got up and started milling around, some filling their plates with food, others gathering in little circles to talk and laugh.

Leora felt out of place. Like she'd told Martha, she was one of the oldest females there. And she was a widow. Most of the girls were in the throes of their first loves, giggling and making eyes, and praying their crushes would wander over and offer them a ride home.

Well, Leora knew who was taking her home, and it had nothing to do with love or courtship or getting to know each other better.

Except ... the way Noah kept glancing at her made her wonder. Was he interested in her? She glanced around as unobtrusively as she could, to see where he was. She spotted him in front of the closed barn door, chatting with Ethel Beiler. Sudden disappointment flashed through her, surprising her. She swallowed and frowned. What was the matter with her anyway? Honestly, a person would think she was interested in Noah King—which she wasn't.

She turned back to one of the girls, Katie, who was chatting with great animation about how cute Justin Bontrager was. Leora smiled and nodded and pretended to be fascinated by it all. But in truth, all she really wanted to do was to go home. She stifled a sigh and wondered when Noah would be ready to go.

She glanced back over at him. He was laughing at something Ethel had said. Looked like it might be awhile. She excused herself from Katie and wandered over to the refreshment table to get something to eat. Not that she was hungry, but it would give her something to do. She chose an egg salad sandwich and a handful of pretzels.

"Is it any *gut*?" asked a voice close to her ear.

She whirled around to stare up at Noah. "Um... I haven't taken a bite yet."

He chuckled. "I see that now. What'd you choose? The egg salad?"

She nodded, raising the half sandwich from her plate like she was toasting him.

"I think I'll have the same." He grabbed a plate and helped himself. He took a bite and nodded appreciatively. "It's nice."

She took a bite and agreed.

"Are you ready to go after you finish eating?" he asked. "Not that I want to hurry you along, mind you."

"I'll be ready. In truth, I'm ready anytime."

He raised his brow. "Are you? Then, let's go."

"*Nee*. Finish your food first. I didn't mean to drag you away before you were ready."

"I'm not that hungry. I'll go out and hitch up Flicker. You can come out to meet me in a few minutes. Does that sound all right?"

She nodded. "Thank you, Noah." She said his name softly and then was embarrassed by how tender her voice sounded. This wouldn't do. She cringed. This wouldn't do at all.

He gave her a curious look before walking away.

She blinked hard. Goodness, but she was going to have to watch herself. Had she become so lonely these days that she would grasp at any possibility for companionship? She was disappointed with herself. She considered herself quite independent, especially for an Amish woman. Secretly, she was proud of that, but the way she was acting now filled her with questions.

She made her way to where everyone's coats and capes had been piled in a heap on a table right inside the barn door. She found hers and pulled it loose.

"You going so soon?" Katie asked, approaching her.

Leora put on a smile. "*Jah*. It's about over anyway."

Katie leaned close. "Not really. Everyone will stay a *gut* while longer to visit." She looked around. "How are you getting home?"

Leora inhaled sharply. She wasn't about to reveal that Noah King was taking her home. That would set the tongues on fire for sure and for certain.

"Oh, I have a ride," she said vaguely, quickly adding, "Have you had a chance to speak to Justin yet?"

Successfully distracted, Katie started in about how she didn't want to appear too forward, but that she was dying to talk to him, and did Leora think it would be all right if Katie went right over to him and said something?

"Definitely," Leora said. "Look, he's standing by himself right now. Why not take that platter of sandwiches from the table and ask him if he wants one? You can pretend you're serving everyone, and then it wouldn't be forward at all."

Katie's face lit up. "*Gut* idea, Leora. Thanks." And without another word, she rushed off.

Leora shook her head with amusement, remembering the days when she had acted in the same manner regarding David. She'd hung onto every word he'd said, every gesture he'd made, everything he did. She had stared at him across the room, praying he'd come and talk to her—just like Katie was doing with Justin.

Ahh, young love.

She balked. Had she grown so old? Was she looking upon young love as something so distant from herself? As if she were an old woman? She was only twenty-four, and here she was observing life as if she were on the tail end of it. She roughly flung her cape around her shoulders and grabbed her scarf, twisting it about her neck.

Had David taken her youth with him? Had his death erased

any further chance for her to find love again? Did she have to stop living because he had?

Her jaw tightened, and she left the barn with her emotions churning. She'd never really looked at it this way before. How had she been acting since David's death? She'd cut herself off from everyone. But hadn't she wanted to? Wasn't that a choice she'd made all by herself?

Noah had the buggy hitched up, and he was coming her way. She hurried and climbed in before he had a chance to open the door for her. She settled herself stoically in the seat and stared straight ahead.

"Are you all right?" Noah asked, clearly sensing her mood.

"I'm fine," she said, her voice clipped.

She heard him sigh but she didn't turn to look at him. He drove the buggy at a steady clip toward her house. The heater was cranking out the heat and she was nearly sweating by the time he rolled up to her porch.

"Here you are, Leora," he said. "Um, thank you for letting me drive you home."

At his words, her shoulders slumped. Honestly, she'd just gone from bad to worse. This nice man had gone out of his way to help her, and she had acted as thankful as a rock. She drew in a long breath and turned toward him.

"I'm sorry, Noah," she said. "I've been terrible company."

He searched her face. "You don't have to be *gut* company," he said. And then he must have realized how his words sounded because she saw his face redden in the glow from the buggy lights. "I mean—"

"I know what you meant," she said, smiling now. "I have been horrible company. I really do appreciate you taking me. And in truth, I had a *gut* time."

"What happened?" he asked. "I, uh, never mind. It's none of my business."

"Katie happened."

"Huh? Katie Gerig?"

Leora was laughing now. "*Jah*. Katie Gerig. And nothing happened. Not really. She was just chatting with me."

Leora could see by his expression that he was thoroughly baffled now.

"Never mind, Noah. Thank you for the ride."

"You're welcome." He jumped out and came around to her side, opening her door for her. She got out.

"Thank you again."

He glanced around. "Do you have enough firewood chopped? Where's your stack?"

She drew back. How odd that he should mention firewood so soon after her conversation with Bill about it earlier.

"It's around the side, and *jah*, I have plenty."

"I'm happy to do some chopping for you, Leora. In truth, I enjoy chopping wood."

She stared at him. Was that true, or was he wanting an excuse to come by? She chastised herself. Did it matter? It was kind of him to offer.

"Thank you, but truly, I have sufficient."

"Will you need a ride to work this week?"

She blinked. "*Nee*. I'm fine. *Gut* night, Noah."

"*Gut* night."

She hurried away, not sure how she felt about him offering to give her rides. When he'd first offered, she hadn't really taken him very seriously, but now, she could see that he was. Was he wanting to court her? She opened the door to her house and slipped inside, shutting the door behind her. In the darkness, she moved to the front window and watched him get back into the buggy.

He was a big man, but he moved with a smoothness that belied his size. His hat was pressed down on his head at a jaunty angle, which gave him a reckless air. But she knew he wasn't reckless at all. He was steady and kind and good.

Did she like him?

She did. He was pleasant to be around, and he hadn't disapproved of her work. But, beyond that? She watched his buggy leave her drive. In truth, she didn't know. She hadn't given such things much thought since before David.

But the idea was interesting, for sure and for certain.

Chapter Six

The colder months on his farm were much slower, and sometimes Noah found himself at loose ends. Thank goodness, the animals still needed tending to, and he'd been working on a new dining table. He wasn't a skilled wood worker, but he did well enough, he supposed. He'd set up a shop of sorts in his barn, and he spent a good deal of time out there. When he finished the table, he thought to make a new headboard for his bed. Keeping busy was important, for he found if he had too much time to spare, his mind would go places he wasn't keen on going.

Like Leora Fisher. And Bill Jeffreys.

Those two were taking entirely too much space in his brain.

"Noah?" came a shrill voice. "Noah King? You in there?"

His barn door inched opened, and Eliza Troyer stuck her head in. "There you are."

He straightened up from sanding the top of the table.

"*Ach*, what are you building?" she asked, wandering inside. "Why, this looks right fine. I didn't know you worked with wood, Noah."

"I'm not very *gut* at it, to be certain," he said.

She ran her mittened hand over the surface of the table. "Looks nice to me." She raised a brow. "I'm sure my niece Doris would be mighty interested in what you're doing out here. I came by to tell you that she's arrived."

Noah held back a groan and half-expected Eliza's niece to pop through the door behind her at any moment. But she wasn't there.

"You must be glad to have her here," he commented.

"Now, I promised to have you over for supper, so I'm here to invite you. Six o'clock this evening and don't be late."

This evening? He wanted to groan out loud, but he held it back.

"Doris is baking up a storm right now. You do like shoofly pie, *ain't so?* I seem to recall that it's one of your favorites. She is really looking forward to meeting you, Noah. And she might be staying a while. Longer than I expected, which suits me just fine. And you'll be happy about it, too, I assure you."

Noah stood there, helpless, in the torrent of her words. Did the woman ever breathe? She answered that question for him by taking a gulping breath.

"You be there, all right? Your place is already set at the table."

He had no choice but to agree. Eliza patted his arm in a matronly way, smiled hugely, and left. He leaned on the table, feeling as if he'd just survived a storm.

So. He was going to supper at the Troyers' that very evening.

With a sigh, he returned to his sanding.

Noah pulled up on the reins in front of the Troyers' house. He supposed he should unhitch Flicker, although he didn't want to. Unhitching the pony meant he would be staying awhile, and he really wanted to escape as quickly as he could. But he knew Eliza Troyer. There would be no early escape from this supper. He got out of his buggy and walked up to Flicker.

"All right, girl. I'll get you unhitched. No reason you should suffer, too." He chuckled.

The front door opened, and Eli Troyer came out. "Eliza said you'd be comin'." He looped his thumbs under his suspenders.

"Hello, Eli," Noah greeted him. "I thought to let Flicker graze a bit."

"You can take her around to the side of the house if you like. There's more grass there. Or you can take her to the barn. It's awful cold out."

"I'll let her graze a bit. Is there a place to tie her up?"

"*Jah.* You'll see the post."

Noah took Flicker around to the corner of the house and secured her to a thin hitching post. He slapped her on the rump. "Enjoy yourself," he muttered, circling back around to the porch.

"Gonna be a cold one tonight," Eli observed. "Ain't a cloud in the sky."

"You're right about that." Noah followed him inside. The blast of warmth from the warming stove nearly knocked him over. It had to be ninety degrees in there.

"Eliza, he's here," Eli called out.

Eliza came bustling from the kitchen. "*Ach*, Eli. So *gut* to see you." She turned back to the kitchen. "Doris, our guest is here. Come on out and greet him."

Doris emerged from the doorway, her dark eyes lit up with some inner fire. "Noah King," she said in a strong voice. "So nice to meet you."

Noah blinked. Doris was beautiful, with wide brown eyes and light brown hair, and a few errant wisps escaping her *kapp*. She was tall and shapely, and her expression was enthusiastic. She wasn't at all what he'd expected. He thought for sure that Doris would be some mousy shy thing who didn't say a word. He wanted to laugh out loud. He should have known better, considering the out-going nature of her aunt.

"Nice to meet you, too," he said, smiling.

"I hope you're *gut* and hungry," she said. "Eliza and I have made enough for half the district, for sure and for certain."

Eliza laughed and gave her niece a playful slap on the shoulder. "Not as much as all that."

Doris winked at Noah. "Don't let her fool you. I suggested we go out and invite all the neighbors up and down the road, but she wouldn't hear of it." She giggled then, a pleasant sound that filled the room.

"You men might as well get seated at the table," Eliza told them. "We're ready."

Eli shrugged and moved to his spot at the head of the table. Noah noted that they'd set a place at the end of the table, likely for him. He sat down there.

"Sure does smell *gut*," he commented.

"Hold your judgement until you taste it," Doris said, disappearing into the kitchen.

Well, this evening might not be so bad after all. Not that Noah was interested in Doris beyond that of being a friend, but still, he'd dreaded this meal all afternoon, and the way it looked now, his dread had been for nothing.

The women brought out the steaming dishes of roast beef, mashed potatoes, gravy, creamed carrots, a basket of fresh biscuits, and a bowl of pickles. Noah's mouth was watering before the silent prayer was led by Eli.

After praying, Eliza started passing the dishes around. Noah took generous helpings of everything.

"Smells *gut* and tastes even better," he remarked between mouthfuls.

Doris flushed with pleasure. "Glad you like it. Shoofly pie for dessert."

"I told him," Eliza said, slathering butter on her biscuit. "It's his favorite."

Talk turned to the weather and the upcoming holidays.

"Where are you spending Thanksgiving?" Eliza asked him.

He hesitated. He was hoping he would be spending it in the company of Leora, but her offhand comment about Martha having plenty of food didn't seem like an official invite. Yet, if he didn't have plans, he knew he was about to. He could see the wheels turning in Eliza's head.

"I've been invited to the meal," he said vaguely.

He should have known he wasn't going to get by with that—not with Eliza.

"Oh? Who invited you?"

"Um, I'll be eating with Martha Yutzi's family," he said, cringing inwardly and hoping he wasn't stretching the truth.

Eliza deflated right before his eyes. "I see." She chewed the edge of her lip. "Why, I think they often have quite a crowd. Perhaps, you'd prefer a smaller setting."

He swallowed. "I wouldn't want to hurt anyone's feelings."

"*Aenti*," Doris said, giving Eliza a look. "You don't want to be interfering with Noah's plans."

He expected Eliza to belt out, "Oh, but I do!" But she didn't say a word. Doris smiled at him.

"I haven't decided how long to extend my visit." She took a drink of milk. "I don't really know Hollybrook all that well. Oh, I've visited here from time to time, but I know there's a lot more here that I haven't seen."

All three of them were staring at him, and he got the message.

"I ... well, I could take you around if you like. Show you the area." He maintained a pleasant expression, but he was annoyed. He was being manipulated, and he didn't like it.

"What a wonderful idea," Eliza gushed. "Noah, you could stop by tomorrow afternoon if you like." She turned to Doris. "You should see the lovely table Noah is making. Perhaps he'll take you by his place and show it to you."

Noah kept his smile fixed. It wasn't that he didn't like Doris. She seemed nice enough, but that Eliza Troyer. Sometimes, she meddled just a bit too much.

"Leave the boy alone," Eli muttered, but his comment was ignored by his wife.

"Doris, I think we're ready for your wonderful dessert," Eliza announced.

With that, the women got up and cleared the table of everything but their glasses of milk and their forks. Within minutes, they were back with two pies and dessert plates.

Doris gave Noah an enormous piece of pie. When they'd all been served, Noah took a bite. It was amazing—the best shoofly pie he'd ever tasted.

"Well?" Eliza asked him.

"It's wonderful *gut*," he said around his mouthful. "Delicious."

Eliza preened as if she'd made the pies. Doris smiled at him and began eating her own piece.

After supper, they adjourned to the front room. Noah kept glancing out the window into the darkness. With how cold it was, he'd expected it to snow, but he supposed the clear skies weren't going to accommodate that. Still, he didn't want to stay too long.

After an hour or so of general chatting, he stood. "I need to be getting on home," he announced. "Thank you for a wonderful meal."

"So soon?" Eliza asked.

"Let the boy be," Eli said, standing also. "I'll see you out."

"*Nee*, I need you in the kitchen, Eli," Eliza said, jumping up.

"What for?"

"There's something funny with the faucet." She smiled at Noah. "Nice to have you over. Doris, can you get the door for him?"

Eliza practically grabbed Eli and dragged him from the room. As soon as they were gone, Doris burst out laughing.

"My subtle *aenti*," she said. "She means well."

Noah smiled. "I s'pose she does."

Doris moved toward the front door and he followed her.

"Now, Noah, I know you're coming for me tomorrow to show me the sights." She paused and laughed again. "Of which I'm sure there are many. Goodness knows how many astounding sights there are in an Amish community..."

He looked at her, not sure if she was making fun of him or her aunt or Hollybrook.

"And of course, it's highly likely that we'll be published

immediately after our ride together..." She batted her eyes at him and then really laughed. "You should see your face, Noah King."

He stood there, not having a clue what to say. This girl was unlike anyone he'd ever met. He had no idea what to think of her.

She leaned close. "Don't fret. I know we're being set up. Truth is, I already have my eye on someone else..."

His brow rose.

"No one you know," she continued. "But someone my *dat* won't approve of. So, we'll just play this game, if it's all right with you. Satisfy my *aenti*."

He smiled then, drawn to her humor.

"And then, poof!" She gestured with her hands like a firework. "It won't have worked out, and I'll go back home."

"All right," he said, grinning. "I'll pick you up about two-thirty tomorrow afternoon. That way, we'll have a *gut* few hours before it turns dark."

Chapter Seven

Despite her continual bravado, Leora didn't want to bicycle to work that day. The weather had turned horribly bitter. She stood on her porch, dreading the ride into town. If it kept up like this, the holidays were going to be white for sure. It wasn't that often that they had snow for Thanksgiving, but it looked like they would this year.

Earlier in the season, she'd heard the men in the district talk about the forecast in the Farmer's Almanac. "Going to be a blistery one, for sure and for certain," old man Stoltzfus had repeated himself more than once. Well, he appeared to be right.

But what choice did Leora have that day? She needed her job because she needed the money. She could hardly phone Bill for a ride when she knew he was preparing orders, though the thought of sitting in his warm truck cab was appealing. He would come for her, too, she was quite sure. But it wouldn't be right. Donna hated filling in as cook, and Leora couldn't do that to her.

And then there was Noah. Since he'd repeatedly offered to drive her, she was certain he was sincere. Maybe, she could ride her bike to his farm and then he could give her a lift in his buggy to town. It would be a much shorter ride for her that way. She took one step down, which took her away from the protection of the porch roof. Was that ice forming in the air?

Was it going to sleet? She could hardly ride in that.

She groaned. This was not going to be pleasant no matter how she approached it. She ran across the gravel drive to the shed where she kept her bike. The ground wasn't slippery yet, so she would likely be all right pedaling as far as Noah's place. This was later than usual for her to be going to work, but Donna had asked her to come in later that day because she wanted to go over orders with her. Evidently, the other waitress for the day didn't get in until three o'clock.

It shouldn't make any difference what time Leora went in anyway. She could arrange her own personal schedule as she wished. She had no one depending on her for anything here at home. She leaned momentarily against the shed door. No. No one depended on her. Not a single soul. The loneliness that she'd been feeling more and more of late rose within her.

David, she thought. *Why did you have to die?*

She shuddered, not willing to follow her thoughts. It did no good. So she was alone. Lots of people were.

Which wasn't exactly true—at least, not in her district.

She pulled open the shed door and retrieved her bicycle, re-shutting the door against the cold. Determined now to take Noah up on his promise, she climbed on her bicycle and pedaled out of her drive and directly toward his house. She hoped he was there, because if he wasn't, she would have to ride even further to get to town since his place was in the opposite direction.

Be there, be there, be there, became the rhythm in her mind and the rhythm of her pedals.

Noah studied the thick gray cloud covering. It didn't look good, but he'd promised Doris to take her for a drive, and he wasn't one to go back on his word. He hitched up Flicker and flipped on the heater in his buggy. He headed back to the barn to pull the door shut.

If it got too slippery, they could cut their drive short. In truth, Noah didn't really know what he was going to show her anyway. It wasn't like there were any fascinating landmarks in the area. He supposed they could just ride around and maybe go through the town of Hollybrook. Nothing really special there, either, but then he didn't think Doris would mind.

If what Doris said was true, they were just playing out a game of sorts anyway. He chuckled. Wouldn't Eliza be hopping mad if she knew all of this was for nothing? Doris already had someone she was sweet on. He wondered why her father would be against the fellow. Was he *Englisch*? If not, what was wrong with him?

Well, none of it was his business.

He was heading back to the buggy when he spotted Leora on her bike. Why, she was turning into his drive. His breath hitched. Was something wrong? Had something happened? He hurried toward her.

"Leora? Is everything all right?"

She jumped off her seat and straddled her bike. "Uh, hello, Noah."

"Hello. Can I help you with something?"

Her eye caught sight of his buggy. "*Ach,* you're going somewhere," she cried.

He followed her gaze and then turned back to her. "I was... Well, I... What is it? Do you need a ride?"

Had she actually come to take him up on his offer? He was so surprised that it left him completely flustered.

"I was..." she said. Then she squared her shoulders and put on a brave smile. "*Nee.* Never mind. I just thought I'd stop and say a quick hello and then be on my way."

She hoisted herself back on the seat and made to ride off.

"Leora ... wait."

She hesitated.

"You need a ride, don't you? You surely didn't come by to say hello."

She slumped a bit. "*Nee,* I don't need a ride. I'll see you later, Noah." She pedaled away.

He ran and caught up with her, grabbing her handlebars, forcing her to stop.

"Leora, you clearly want a ride. Are you going into town? To your job?"

She blinked and she looked so vulnerable in that moment, that he had to stifle an urge to take her in his arms. But the moment passed, and she smiled at him. "I am going to my job, and I need to hurry, or I'll be late."

"Because you rode out of your way to see if I'd give you a ride, *ain't so?*" His voice was gentle.

Her eyes misted over with tears, but she blinked them away. "You're clearly going somewhere. You're busy, and I'm fine. Now, please let go of my bicycle, and I'll be on my way."

"Get off," he told her. "Come on. Climb off."

She gripped the handlebars more tightly. "I won't. Now, let me be on my way."

"Leora Fisher, I'm not joking around with you. Get off this bicycle. I'll put it in my barn and give you a ride to work." He wasn't about to let her ride off. She'd actually come to take him up on his offer.

"B-but you are going somewhere."

"I am," he said, dreading that she would know what he was doing, but there was no help for it. "We'll pick up Doris on the way to Hollybrook."

"Doris?" There was hesitation in her voice.

"Eliza Troyer's niece from Linder Creek. Now, hurry up, or you will be late."

In truth, he was surprised when she actually got off the bicycle. Goodness, but she was a stubborn one. He knew she was mulling over why he would be picking up Eliza's niece, but she didn't question him. She just climbed off her bike and stood there while he ran it back to his barn. When he emerged, he called her over.

"Why are you still standing out in the cold?" he asked. "Climb in. The heater's on."

She trudged to the buggy, clearly still reluctant to accept his ride. He hurried around to open the door for her, but she beat him to it, climbing over the front seat to get in the back.

"You can sit up here," he told her.

"*Nee.* I'll leave it for Doris."

"Do you know her?"

"*Nee.*" She pressed her lips tightly together, obviously not wanting to converse further.

By then, he was deeply regretting his promise to Doris. He would be much happier just taking Leora to work.

"What time do you get off?" he asked.

"I'm not sure..."

"*Jah*, you are. What time?"

She shrugged. "I don't need a ride home."

He tensed. Of course, she wouldn't need a ride home—Bill Jeffreys would take her home.

"Sure, you need a ride. If you don't tell me what time, I'll just show up in a couple hours and wait for you. I s'pose I could sit and order a cup of coffee and sip it for however long it takes."

She laughed then, and it was like the birds had suddenly come out in spring. He glanced at her, grinning.

"You're stubborn, *ain't so?*" she said.

"No more than you."

She shook her head. "I'll probably work for three hours."

"I'll be there."

"But what about Doris?"

"I'll have her back to Eliza's by then."

He could see the increased curiosity in her eyes and for some reason, it pleased him. He didn't mind at all if Leora Fisher wondered about him and Doris. Suppressing a smile, he directed the buggy toward the Troyers' place.

When they arrived, he bounded out to go to knock on the door, but before he could, Doris came out. She looked pretty in her deep blue cape and knitted scarf. Her cheeks were rosy as if she'd already been out in the cold.

"Hello, Noah," she said. She looked beyond him toward the buggy. "Do we have another person joining us?"

She didn't sound disappointed exactly, but there was something in her voice that he couldn't detect.

"It's Leora Fisher. She needs a ride to work in Hollybrook, so I thought we'd start our tour there."

Doris raised her brows but didn't say anything. She went down the steps in front of him and got to the buggy first. He joined her as she was settling into her seat. She turned and looked at Leora.

"Hello, I'm Doris. Noah tells me you're Leora."

Leora nodded. "Nice to meet you, Doris."

"You, too." Doris turned back around and smiled at Noah. "Lead on, tour guide." And then, she laughed.

Doris kept up a stream of chatter the entire way to Jeffreys Diner. Noah noted that Leora kept silent, only answering if she were asked something. He glanced back at her a time or two, trying to read her mood, but she wouldn't look at him. When they arrived at the diner, Doris got out to let Leora out.

Noah got out, too, and followed Leora to the door of the diner.

"I'll be back in three hours," he said.

"No need," Leora answered. "I'll find my own way home."

She reached out to pull the door to the diner open, but he blocked her with his arm.

"I'll be here," he said, standing a bit taller. In truth, he was surprised as his insistence. He usually wasn't quite this forthright, but the very idea of her getting a ride with Bill Jeffreys made his throat burn.

She looked up at him, her blue eyes snapping. "We'll see," was all she said.

He dropped his arm, and she disappeared into the diner. He went back to the buggy and got in.

"Hmm," said Doris. "I'm thinking that *Aenti* Eliza got it all wrong."

"What do you mean?"

"She told me you didn't have a girl, but I think she's mistaken."

He felt his cheeks go warm. "She's not my girl." *Not yet, anyway.*

"Oh, but I think she is." Doris hit him on the arm with the back of her hand. "She seems nice..."

He cocked a brow.

"And awful quiet." Doris laughed. "Course I s'pose I didn't give her much of a chance to speak."

He chuckled. "*Nee,* you didn't."

She smiled. "I like to talk." She peered out the side window. "Hollybrook looks nice enough. You live here your whole life?"

"*Jah.*"

"I've lived in Linder Creek my whole life. In truth, I wouldn't mind trying something new."

"And your beau? Is he in Linder Creek?"

A shadow passed over her face, but it cleared quickly. "My beau?" She licked her lips. "Um, I guess so."

He frowned. "You guess so? What does that mean?"

"He's, um, detained elsewhere right now."

"Detained?" This was getting interesting. Noah couldn't imagine how a man might be detained.

"He'll be back in one month or so," she said, folding her hands on her lap.

"Where is he?"

She cleared her throat. "He's in prison."

Noah jerked up on the reins and poor Flicker came to a jolting stop.

"What?"

"You heard me full well," she said crisply.

He hesitated. "I, uh, guess that's why your dat wouldn't approve."

She nodded and tears came to her eyes.

"I'm sorry. It ain't my business, but why is he in prison?"

She sighed. "He made a stupid decision."

Noah waited.

74

She sighed again. "Fine. He borrowed an *Englisch* friend's car..."

"Borrowed?"

She sighed. "He took it without permission. He was going to bring it back. Trouble was, the so-called friend didn't see it that way. But his record was clean, and the judge was merciful, so he didn't get a long sentence."

Noah had never known anyone who'd been to prison. He couldn't imagine having a *beau* in prison. What in the world would that be like? And why had the fellow done such a dumb thing in the first place? Well, he likely had some kind of reason...

Doris was watching him. "I can't believe it..." she murmured.

"Can't believe what?"

"I expected to see you get all judgy when I told you. Most folks do. In fact, most folks are scandalized. Everyone in my district would be, that's for sure and for certain. I get weary of it. My *mamm* is the worst of all. She simply can't accept the fact that I still love Jordan and am waiting for him."

"I see. And your *dat* doesn't know you love him? You said he *wouldn't* approve."

"He might suspect it. My *mamm* is too afraid to tell him. Besides, she thinks my feelings will disappear. Go away. Like they'd never been there at all. Thus, her shipping me to *Aenti* Eliza's house. You know, in an effort to see me rid of Jordan. And to foist me onto you." She gave a sardonic laugh. "Sorry about that."

"No need to be sorry." But he did feel sorry for her. He knew what it was to love someone and not have them. "When he gets out, what then?"

"I assume he'll come back to Linder Creek. His folks will take him in. And then I hope he'll start courting me—official-like, you know?"

"I'm sure he will." Noah snapped the reins and they got underway again.

"You're not asking for all the details."

He laughed. "I am wondering, though. But I figure if you want to tell me, you will." He looked at her and smiled. "It's not like you don't enjoy talking."

She burst into laughter at that comment. "You're right on that. Truth is, I don't know what he was thinking that night. I don't even know all the details. My folks prohibited me from speaking with him after he was arrested, even not knowing at the time how I felt about him. So, I only heard snippets of information. None of it made much sense. But I know Jordan. He had to have had a good reason for what he did. I'll find out soon."

"You been writing to him?"

"As much as I can. My *mamm* is keeping a tight leash on me."

"Have you written since you got here?"

She grinned. "*Jah*. But he doesn't dare send me mail here. *Aenti* would have a heart attack."

Noah laughed, turning the buggy down a side road. "That she would," he agreed.

Chapter Eight

Leora hung up her cape and took off her mittens and scarf. She sat down at her work desk and methodically removed her ledger from the top drawer. She sat stiffly and stared at the pages. Why was she so annoyed? She'd gotten a ride—and in a warm buggy. Noah had been nothing but nice, and so had that Doris girl. Leora hadn't needed to ride to town in the freezing cold, worrying about sliding if sleet began to fall.

She'd been safely delivered with a promise of a ride home.

So, what was her problem? Because her annoyance seemed to be growing by the minute. She ground her teeth. She was acting the fool. And how ungrateful could a person be?

"Thank you, thank you, thank you," she muttered to herself, trying to switch her mood.

"For what?" came a voice from the door.

She looked up. Bill stood there, wiping his hands on his white apron and grinning at her. "Have I done something nice and I don't know it?"

Her face burned with embarrassment. "*Nee*," she said. "I was just... I was just thinking of something."

"Well if you have unclaimed gratitude, I'll take it."

She shook her head, already feeling better. Bill's smile and humor were always a good idea.

"You didn't ride your bike, did you?"

"*Nee*. I got a ride."

He straightened. "With Noah? Did he bring you?"

She knew her cheeks were flushed; although, why she should be flustered in front of him, she couldn't fathom. "*Jah*. He did."

"Oh."

"Doris was with us," she blurted.

He raised a brow. "Doris?"

"*Jah*. Noah was taking her for a drive."

Bill looked highly pleased with this bit of information. He stepped inside her office. "So, you'll need a ride home, then?"

"Um, Noah is coming to get me in three hours."

"With Doris?"

"I-I don't know," she said, even though Noah had clearly told her he'd have Doris back to Eliza's by then.

"You know my offer still stands." He walked to her desk, and his presence seemed to suck the air out of the room. Her heart rate increased, and she prayed she hadn't turned bright red.

"I-I know."

"It *always* stands, Leora." He traced his finger along the edge of her desk.

"Thank you," she said, now completely flustered. She swallowed hard and stared at the ledger page. "I should get to work."

"Of course," he said. "I know Donna wanted to work with you sometime today. I think her help is coming in at three. Does Donna know you're here?"

Leora looked up at him. "She saw me come in."

"All right, then. I better get to work, too." He gave her a beaming smile and left her office.

Alone, she drew in a huge breath. This was an odd day. Very, very odd. She shivered and then with great intent, focused on the work before her.

Donna stood and scooted back the chair she'd brought into Leora's office. "I think that does it for this order, Leora," she said. "Thanks for coming in today."

"Of course," Leora answered. "I'll get these orders out before I leave."

Donna checked her watch. "Don't work too late. Do you have a ride home?"

"Noah King is supposed to be coming to get me."

"Noah King? I think I know who he is. Does he have brown hair and really dark brown eyes? About so tall?" She gestured with her hand. "And he often wears a dark green shirt?"

Donna could have been describing half the guys in her district.

But then she said, "And the most beautiful smile I've ever seen in my life?"

"*Jah.* That's him," Leora agreed. So, she wasn't the only one who noticed how Noah's smile seemed to encompass his entire face, or how even and white his teeth were, or how his eyes crinkled with mirth when he did smile. In truth, Noah's smile was one of the nicest things about him.

"Is he your beau?" Donna asked.

"What? Uh, *nee. Nee*, I... Of course not," she finished,

wondering why in the world she was stammering so. She was a widow. She didn't have a beau.

"I see. Has Bill met him?"

"*Jah,* just the other day."

Donna nodded and then put on a smile. "Well, you've been here for almost three hours. Why not have Noah come on in and have a cup of hot chocolate before he takes you home?"

Leora swallowed, not wanting to invite Noah in at all. At that point, all she wanted to do was go home, but she could hardly be rude. Not when Donna was always so kind to her.

"I'll ask him to," she said.

"Good. I'd like to formally meet him," Donna said. And with that, she left Leora's office.

Leora sank back into her chair. If Noah came in, then Bill would come out, and they would have another awkward exchange. She groaned. If only she had enough money to buy a buggy and keep a horse of her own. But she'd been forced to sell both after David died. Just like she'd been forced to sell off so many things they'd owned.

Well, there was nothing for it now. Maybe in time, she could find more work and save up her money. She could buy a pony cart first; they were less expensive. Less protection in the cold, too, but safer than bicycling in this weather.

She stared at the phone sitting on her desk. Even after all these months, it was still odd to make frequent calls, but this was business, so it was allowed. She picked up the phone and dialed one of the diner's suppliers, the list of items needed in her hand.

A half hour later, Donna came to her doorway. "He's here, Leora."

"Okay," Leora said. She'd already put everything away and was ready to go. But she didn't put on her cape; she hurried through the restaurant and outside. She could see that Noah was indeed alone, and she felt relief spread through her. She went to his window.

"You aren't ready? Shall I wait out here?" he asked.

"Donna Jeffreys wants you to come in for a cup of hot chocolate. Do you have time?"

He answered right away. "Sure. Let me secure Flicker. Go on back in, Leora. You'll catch your death out here."

She was already shivering, so she did as she was bidden. A minute later, he came inside to the tinkling of the bell. Donna came right up to them.

"Donna, as you know, this is my friend Noah King. Noah, this is Donna Jeffreys," Leora introduced them.

Noah inclined his head. "Nice to meet you formally, Donna. I've seen you before when I've come in."

"Yes. I recognize you, too. Nice to meet you. Sit right over here. I'll bring you the hot chocolate right away." She looked at Noah. "Are you hungry? Would you like something else?"

"*Nee*," Noah said. "Hot chocolate sounds right nice about now."

Noah sat across the booth from Leora.

"Nice person," he said, watching Donna head for the kitchen.

"*Jah*. She's real nice."

He folded his hands on the table, and she could see the callouses on the sides of his fingers.

"How was work?" he asked.

"Fine."

His eyes were studying her, and she felt uncomfortable. She searched her mind for something to say, but before she could think of anything, Bill was walking toward them.

"Noah King, we meet again," he said, his hand outstretched.

They shook hands, and then Bill turned to her. "When are you coming in again, Leora?"

"I need to follow up on some orders tomorrow, so I'll be here in the morning for a couple hours."

"I'll be picking you up. Will nine o'clock work?"

Inwardly, she sighed. Why was he doing this? It was like he was challenging Noah somehow, and she didn't like it.

"Not necessary," she said. "I have a ride."

Both men stared at her. She did her best not to squirm under their scrutiny. In truth, the only ride she had was her bicycle, but she wasn't going to admit that.

"You do?" Noah asked first.

"I do. Now, I don't want to talk about it any further. Is the hot chocolate ready?" she asked Bill.

He blinked, and she saw the surprise on his face. She wasn't usually curt, and she could see he was annoyed.

"I'll go check," he said, and despite the look on his face, his voice was gracious.

"Thank you," she murmured.

When he left, she avoided Noah's gaze. She knew he was looking at her, she could feel it. She licked her lips and then turned back to him. "How was Doris's tour? Did she like Hollybrook?"

She wondered just how chummy they'd gotten on the drive, but she could hardly ask that.

"It was *gut*. She liked the town well enough."

"How long is she staying?"

"I don't know for sure. Likely through Thanksgiving at least."

"Oh." So, Doris was staying a few weeks then. Leora wasn't sure how she felt about that, but then, it was hardly her business.

Donna came out with two steaming cups of chocolate. She put them down and said, "Enjoy."

"We sure will," Noah responded pleasantly. "Thank you, Donna."

Leora put her hands around the mug, soaking in the heat. It smelled divine, and she saw that Donna had dropped a few marshmallows into each cup. Noah took a drink of his.

"*Ach*, it's hot. Be careful," he said.

She took a tiny sip of hers. It was hot, but it felt good on her throat, sending warmth through her. She took another sip.

Noah looked around the diner. "It's quite busy in here."

"It usually is," Leora said, happy to have something to talk about. "The weekends are even busier. Sometimes, people have to wait for a table."

"They've owned this place for a long time, *ain't so?*"

"I'm not sure exactly how long. But over five years, I think."

Noah took another drink of his chocolate. "I'm glad it's doing well. It seems like some businesses just get started in town, and they're closed again just as quick-like."

"Like that home decorating place? I forget what it was called."

"Divine Rooms?"

She smiled. "*Jah*. That was it. I don't think they were open more than four or five months."

"You're right on that."

"A dream that died," she murmured, bending over her cup and letting the steam rise to her face.

"What?"

"I just said, a dream that died."

He nodded, looking pensive. "That's always sad."

Yes, it was. She thought of the dreams that had died with David. Her eyes burned and she blinked rapidly, not wanting Noah to see the tears in her eyes. But it was too late. He reached across the table and put his hand over hers—for no more than a second or two.

"I'm sorry about your dreams, Leora," he said softly.

Her throat tightened and for a moment, she feared she might burst into tears right there in the middle of the diner. She cleared her throat and shook her head. "It's over now. But thank you."

"I was right sorry when I heard the news about your husband." His dark brown eyes were steady on hers. "I wish I could have done something to help you."

Her forehead creased. She hadn't even been aware of him when it had happened. The people came and went in a blur at her farm. She'd only really noticed Martha. Martha had stayed with her day and night during those days of the viewing and the funeral. Martha had handled so many things. Had Noah King even come to David's funeral? She had no idea.

More than likely, he had, though. Funerals were times when everyone in the district was glad to be together. Glad to catch up with each other. Glad to take a break from their usual chores and routine. Glad to share another community meal.

"You moved houses so quickly afterward, Leora. I was worried."

Her frown deepened. "You were?" she asked, stunned.

His face turned red, and he coughed. "All of us were."

Worried? She didn't think that was the right term. She didn't feel their worry; she felt their censure when she sold the farm so quickly. She felt their curiosity. She'd been the main topic of talk for quite some time afterward.

"Thank you," was all she said now.

They drank the rest of their hot chocolate in silence. It wasn't awkward, and Leora began to relax. The chocolate tasted good, and she thought that she should really make hot chocolate for herself more often at home. Sometimes, she got tired of tea. When she finished her cup, she pushed it gently away.

"You ready?" he asked.

She nodded, and they both stood.

"Let me go pay for this."

"You don't have to. I'm sure Donna doesn't expect it."

"Still, I need to offer."

She watched him cross the diner and speak with Donna, who was busy at the register. *Noah is a good man,* she thought again. She wondered if he would be seeing Doris again. Doris certainly had seemed an amusing person to be around. Did he like her? Did he like amusing people? Leora didn't feel very amusing these days.

She blanched. What was she doing? Trying to discern whether Noah liked her or not? Her cheeks went hot and she turned aside, staring out the large window into the cold outdoors. She saw Noah's buggy, saw Flicker paw the ground, saw the billows of steam coming from the horse's nostrils.

"You were right," Noah said from behind her. "She wouldn't let me pay."

Leora bundled up quickly, and together, they left the diner. She was almost certain Bill was watching them from the kitchen, but she didn't turn to check. The frigid air affronted them the minute they stepped outside.

"*Ach,* it'll be cold tonight," Noah said, rubbing his hands together and looking to the sky. He opened her door for her, and she climbed in.

He got in on his side and flipped the switch on his heater. "I should have had this warming up," he told her apologetically.

"It's fine," she said, smiling. "In truth, I still marvel at these heaters. Goodness, but they make a difference."

"That is true," he agreed. "Imagine our poor cold ancestors." He laughed, and she joined him.

They got underway, and she gazed out at the businesses they were passing. Some of them had window displays for Thanksgiving, full of cornucopias, pumpkins and squash, and pilgrims. Other stores seemed to have skipped Thanksgiving entirely and already had Christmas decorations up.

"Leora?"

She turned to him. "*Jah?*"

"I'll pick you up tomorrow morning about eight-thirty. Will that suit?"

She tensed, staring at him. He'd seen through her earlier claim —he knew she didn't really have a ride. He knew she'd been referring to her bicycle.

"How... How did you—"

"How did I know you didn't have a ride?" he cut in. "Because I'm beginning to know you, Leora."

His words filled the buggy with a sense of intimacy that flustered her. He didn't know her, not really. But the fact that he'd seen through her comment was unnerving—and comforting at the same time.

She swallowed and then blew out her breath. "Eight-thirty will be fine," she muttered.

He grinned at her and turned his attention back to his horse.

Chapter Nine

After dropping Leora off at her house, Noah went straight home. When he pulled into his drive, he noted that he had company.

Eliza jumped out of her buggy and stood there waiting for him. He groaned and pulled up beside her. Instead of waiting for him to get out, she climbed straight into his buggy.

"Doris tells me that you probably won't go riding together anymore."

He frowned. "Did she?"

"And why aren't you? Doris is a lovely girl. Surely, you can see that."

He stifled a moan. "*Jah*. She's a lovely girl."

"You courting someone I don't know about?" she asked, her chest heaving.

He thought of Leora. But in truth, they weren't courting... Not yet.

"*Nee*, I'm not courting anyone."

Eliza leaned close, studying his face. "I know these things are kept secret. Are you telling me the truth?"

"Why are you so fired up about Doris and me?" he asked, still holding the reins tightly.

"Why wouldn't I be? You're a fine young man, and she's a fine young lady." Eliza shrugged casually, as if poking her nose into other people's romantic affairs was completely normal—which it wasn't. "And then Doris could move to Hollybrook, which would suit me right fine."

"You want us to court so she'll move to Hollybrook?"

Eliza sighed and her entire body deflated. "That ain't all of it."

He waited.

"I promised her *mamm*, my sister, that I'd see to it that she found a young man here."

Thoughts of Doris's beau behind bars flitted through his mind. "I see."

Eliza put her hand on his arm. "Doris needs a distraction," she said earnestly. "I promised my sister."

"So, you decided on me."

"Don't say it that way. I'm doing you a favor, can't you see? Doris is lovely."

"But we won't be courting," he told her.

She scowled. "Take her for a ride again. Give this some time."

"She isn't interested in me," he said gently, not bothering to tell her that his heart, too, was elsewhere.

"She could be..."

He didn't respond.

"*Ach*, for goodness sakes," Eliza said, grabbing the handle of the door. "Did she say anything to you? Anything about another young man?"

Eliza was clearly referring to Doris's friend in jail, but he didn't feel right talking about it.

"Eliza, I'm sorry I can't help you."

She sniffed with great annoyance and got out. "Thank you anyway, Noah King," she sputtered and stomped off.

He couldn't help but shake his head and give a rueful smile. He understood Eliza's heart. She cared about Doris, and she cared about her sister. She was trying to do something good for everyone. And indeed, Doris was a fine person.

Just not the person for him.

Someone was banging on her door. Snuggled in bed, Leora groaned and wriggled to a sitting position. What was going on? Was that her door? Had something horrible happened? She lit a candle and stumbled to her front door and pulled it open.

"You all right?" Tom Yutzi asked.

"*Jah*, of course, I am. What's going on?"

"Martha made me come over to check on you."

"Why? It's the middle of the night! What's happened?"

"The Yoder's barn is burning."

Leora lifted the candle higher and saw the soot on Tom's face and clothes.

"*Ach!* I'll get dressed."

"*Nee*. Just lock your door, will you?"

She stared at him in confusion. "But I can help."

"The fire trucks are there. They're putting it out."

"But I can—"

"Someone started it, Leora. Sam Yoder saw someone running away from his barn."

"*What?*"

It wasn't the first time Amish folk had been targeted for arson. But never, never had it happened in Hollybrook.

"Martha made me come check on you. Sorry to wake you up. I didn't want to disturb you, but Martha is in a stew. I knew she wouldn't rest until she knew you were fine. Now lock your doors."

"But I don't have a barn. I only have the shed. I'm in no danger."

He shrugged as if that didn't matter. "Lock your doors."

"I will, Tom."

And just that quickly, he was gone.

Leora stood there, staring after him into the darkness. Someone had set Sam's barn on fire? Were his animals safe? And was the house spared? She shivered as the cold from outside crept into her house. Quickly, she shut the door and locked it. Most folks in their district didn't lock anything up.

Once she'd moved to this house, Leora had started locking her doors. After burying her husband, she felt oddly vulnerable in her new place, and at first, she felt better when she was locked in. But lately, she'd gone back to her old ways, leaving everything unlocked.

Now fully awake, she wandered into her kitchen and got a drink of water. *Arson?* Were they sure? And what was wrong with people? Why would someone do such a thing?

They'd be having a barn raising soon, and it would be all the more difficult in this weather. But the Yoders could hardly go through the winter with no barn. This had to be most upsetting to them. She would go over later that morning and take some food.

Wait. Noah was coming at eight-thirty to take her to work. She could have him swing by on the way, if that was all right with him. She wondered whether he was over at the Yoders right now. Probably. News could spread through their district at unbelievable speed, even without phones. Likely, every able-bodied man was over there.

She sat down at her table and set the candle in front of her. What time was it, anyway? She held the candle up and the circle of light reached the clock above her sink. Two o'clock. And here she was wide awake. She might as well bake something for the Yoders now. It would be better than tossing and turning and trying to go back asleep.

She could bake the Yoders some biscuits and a cake. She stood up and lit the lantern she kept on the counter. Its light filled the room, and she blew out the candle. She rummaged through her cupboards getting out all the ingredients she needed. Then she turned on her cook stove to preheat.

It was cold in the house. The fire she'd banked in the heating stove before turning in must have gone out. She went to put another log on it and then remembered she needed to bring in another load of logs from outside under the roof overhang.

She stood, debating. Should she go outside right then and fetch the logs?

She remembered the look on Tom's sooty face. Was whoever started the fire still about? She shuddered. Surely not. And besides, a person who started fires wasn't likely a person who would hurt someone. They were two different things entirely. Weren't they?

Leora moved to the side door and put her hand on the knob, but she didn't turn it. An unreasonable fear took hold of her. *Ach,* but this was silly. She turned the knob, but she still didn't pull the door open. She drew in a long breath.

No. She wouldn't go outside in the night. She would just work in the cold.

She re-checked the lock and went back to the kitchen counter. Her hands trembled slightly as she began measuring out the cups of flour.

Chapter Ten

Leora was perched on the arm of her couch, craning her neck to see outside when Noah showed up the next morning. She was completely ready—bundled up with her baked goods tucked into a basket. When the buggy came to a stop, she got up, grabbed her basket and went outside.

Noah was just climbing out.

"*Ach*, Leora, you're ready."

"I am," she answered. He looked tired. "Were you at the Yoders last night?"

His eyes widened. "I was. You heard about the fire."

"*Jah*. Tom Yutzi came by in the middle of the night."

Noah took her basket from her. "He did? Why?"

"Martha was worried about me."

He nodded slowly. "Everyone is a bit skittish. So then, you know the fire was set."

"Tom told me."

Noah opened her side of the buggy and placed the basket behind her seat. "It's happened in other districts."

"But never ours."

"*Nee.* Never ours."

She climbed into the buggy, but before Noah could shut the door, she put her hand on his arm. "Do you think it was a one-time thing?"

"I pray so."

"You don't think the person will come around and set more fires?"

Noah looked deeply into her eyes. She dropped her hand, but she didn't take her eyes from his.

"Are you worried, Leora?" His voice was soft.

She blinked. "Um, *nee. Nee.* I'm fine."

"It's all right, you know. You're entitled to be concerned..."

"*Nee,*" she said quickly, embarrassed now. "I-I just wondered is all."

He didn't move, and his gaze stayed fixed on her. The cold outside air wafted into the buggy, mingling with the heat pooling close to her feet.

"You have locks on your doors?" he asked.

"*Jah*. Of course."

"And you use them?"

"Tom told me to lock up last night."

"He's right. It's a *gut* idea."

"Uh, we better get going. I thought maybe we could stop by the Yoders. I have some baked goods for them."

He glanced behind her to the basket he'd put on the floor. "That was right nice of you."

She shrugged. "I was awake..."

"You baked in the middle of the night?"

"*Jah*."

He shook his head and smiled. "If I'd known you were up and baking, I'd have stopped by for a bite." He laughed and then seemed to realize what he'd said, and his face turned red. He backed away. "You're right. We'd better get underway, or you'll be late for work."

He shut her door and went around to his side. They started down the road, and it didn't take long to arrive at the Yoders' place. Noah turned the buggy up the drive, and Leora suppressed a gasp. What was left of the barn stood like a hulking shadow of charred wood. Most of the walls had crumpled, leaving only some beams and a jagged portion of roof. The ground was heaped with blackened chunks of wood and ashes. The ground around the barn looked soggy and grooved with tire tracks, probably left by the fire trucks.

She put her hand to her mouth and shook her head. "It's gone," she whispered. "Burned to the ground."

Noah was solemn as he said, "*Jah*. Nothing left to salvage."

It was as if they were driving through a cemetery, slowly and almost reverently. Noah's eyes were misted over, and Leora held back her own tears.

"The animals?" she asked, fearing the answer.

"They're safe."

She exhaled with relief. When they neared the house, Ellen Yoder stepped out onto the porch. She wiped her hands down her apron. Her face was ragged, and it looked as if she hadn't slept in days. Leora grabbed the basket from behind her seat and got out.

"*Ach*, Ellen, I'm so sorry," she said, going to Ellen and giving her a hug. "How are you faring?"

"We're all safe, thanks be to *Gott*."

"Noah tells me that your animals are safe, too."

Ellen nodded and wiped a tear from her eye. "*Jah*. We got them all out."

"I brought you some baked goods," Leora said, holding out the basket.

Ellen took it with a smile. "Thank you, Leora. That was kind of you."

"It was the least I can do. When will the barn raising be?"

"I don't rightly know. The bishop will be coming by later this morning. Truth is, we aren't supposed to touch the ruins until an inspector goes through. They're looking for clues, I s'pose."

"It's hard to believe someone would do such a thing."

Ellen blew out her breath. "We must pray for them. A person like that has got to be hurting."

"I think you're right."

"People were mighty upset last night," she went on. "It gives a person an unsettled feeling. You know, to think someone is out there..."

"I locked my doors last night and when I left the house this morning."

"You know, Leora, we try to live apart from the world and worldly things. But sometimes, the world invades us."

Leora had never heard it put quite like that. It gave her an uneasy feeling, but she agreed, thought she didn't like to think about it.

"We'll just continue praying for *Gott's* protection," Leora said.

"Can you come in for a few minutes?" Ellen offered.

"*Nee.* I'm on my way into town for some errands," she said, and then she corrected herself. "Actually, I'm on my way to work at Jeffreys Diner."

There. Her friend Martha couldn't accuse her of being mysterious right then. She wondered if Ellen would question her about her job, but she was clearly too distracted, which was understandable.

"*Gut* bye, Ellen. Give your husband my greetings."

"I will. He's fast asleep sitting in his chair in the front room. Thank you for coming by and for the food."

"I'll be here with more food on the day of the barn raising," Leora told her and turned to go.

Back in the buggy, Noah smiled at her. "I bet she was right glad to get the food."

"Seemed so," Leora said, her mind still coming to grips with the blackened pile of what used to the Yoders' barn. How many times had she attended preaching service in that barn? She couldn't remember. But she'd always liked their barn. It was more airtight, making it warmer in the winter months. And Sam Yoder kept it spotless, which was no small task.

Well, they'd soon have another barn, their district would see to that.

"Has the bishop been by yet?" Noah asked. "When's the barn raising?"

"She doesn't know, but the bishop is coming soon."

"News will spread quickly," Noah said. "It'll be arranged by nightfall, for sure and for certain."

Leora nodded, settling back for the ride into Hollybrook. But they were stopped on the way, when another buggy pulled them over on a wide spot in the road.

"Any more information on the fire?" Henry Lapp called out through his buggy window.

"Nothing new," Noah said. "How are you doing, Henry?"

"A bit tired from last night is all. The missus was plenty upset. I had to practically keep vigil the rest of the night to make sure no one set our barn on fire."

"Nasty business," Noah said.

"You're right at that," Henry said. "It's got everyone on edge. I hope the *Englischers* get it figured out before anything else happens."

"I'm sure nothing more will happen."

"I hope you're right, Noah." Henry craned his neck. "Leora Fisher? That you? *Gut* morning."

She leaned around Noah. "*Gut* morning, Henry."

She cringed, wondering what gossip would follow this meeting. Now, folks would think she and Noah were courting.

"We'll be seeing you around," Noah said, snapping his reins again. When they were underway, he turned to her. "Sorry about that."

"About what?" she asked.

"I could see it bothered you for Henry to notice we were riding together."

"*Nee.* It doesn't matter," she said, but she was lying. It most certainly did matter. She didn't want people getting the wrong idea. She analyzed her thoughts for a moment. What difference did it really make what people thought? It didn't change what was. And she and Noah were not courting—no matter what conclusion others might come to.

And would it be so bad if they were? She shuddered, not comfortable with where her thoughts were taking her. She wasn't courting anyone. She was a widow, and she still missed her husband.

But did that mean she couldn't fall in love again? Did it?

She pressed her lips together in a fine line. She needed to put her mind elsewhere.

Chapter Eleven

Bill Jeffreys was on the floor of the diner when she entered. His gaze immediately went beyond her to Noah's buggy pulling away from the curb.

"Noah give you a ride again?" he questioned.

She flushed. "*Jah*."

He stepped toward her. "We heard about what happened last night. It's all over town. I assume they were friends of yours."

She nodded. "*Jah*. The Yoders. *Gut* people."

"Did they catch who set the fire?"

"*Nee*."

"I heard everyone was all right. And that the animals got out of the barn safely. Is that true?"

She nodded again.

He gave a low whistle and shook his head. "I can hardly believe someone would do that. What motivation could they have had? It's not like you folks go around making problems."

"No motivation is needed," she said. "Some people fear us. We're different. That makes us a threat in some people's eyes. You'd be surprised what has happened at times."

He took her arm and pulled her toward a spot against the wall where the fountain drinks were poured. "Like what?"

She frowned. "You really want to know?"

"I really want to know."

Donna breezed by, greeting Leora with a smile.

"Some customers just came in," she told her brother over her shoulder. "I'll have an order for you in a minute."

"I'll be ready," he answered. He looked down at Leora. "Like what?"

"Like trying to run us off the road sometimes. Like throwing rocks at us in our buggies—"

"*What?*" He cut her off.

She shrugged. "It happens."

"I had no idea. I'm so sorry."

"It wasn't you who did it," she said.

"Still…"

"And there's all the gawking and pointing at us and sneaking to take photos of us, like we're ignorant and don't know it's happening." She gave him a rueful smile. "Not that any of that is dangerous like setting a barn on fire."

He squeezed her arm. "You must think non-Amish people are terrible."

She shook her head. "*Nee*. We don't. Most *Englischers* I know —*we* know—are fine folks."

He lowered his head to speak more directly to her. "Am I included in that? Am I one of the fine folks?"

She felt there was more behind the question than the actual words he used, and she squirmed a bit, stepping back.

"Of course," she finally said. "You and your sister are kind and *gut* people."

He laughed, his face alight with amusement. Just then, his sister came over with an order. He listened to her, and after smiling once more at Leora, he disappeared into the kitchen.

It was only a few hours later that Leora realized her mistake. She hadn't made arrangements for Noah to pick her up, nor had he asked when she'd be ready. The fire had clearly shaken both of them up. But now, she was ready to go home, and she would have to walk. She sighed, wishing she had her bicycle. It would have been cold and uncomfortable, but a far sight better than walking.

Still, she had no other choice. Even if she were to call the closest shanty to Martha's house, there was no reason for Martha to be listening to messages at that precise time on that precise day.

Leora was stuck. And she didn't want to ask Bill Jeffreys for a ride.

She bundled up in her cape and scarf and mittens and headed out of her office. Bill stood behind the steaming griddle, looking completely preoccupied, so she didn't even bid him farewell. If she did, he'd probably ask her how she was getting home, and he was entirely too busy for her to impose on his good graces.

She went onto the floor and caught Donna's eye. Leora waved good-bye to her and slipped from the diner. The cold November air bit at her cheeks as she turned to head home. She figured it would likely take her about two hours to walk home. She shrank further inside her cape and increased her speed. She could probably cut off about fifteen minutes if she walked fast.

At least her feet were warm, and that was something. Her heavy woolen socks and sturdy black shoes worked well in the winter. They were only inadequate if there was a lot of snow on the ground. They'd already had snow that year, but it was mostly melted now, leaving only occasional dirty clumps scattered about. But the temperature had to be hovering near freezing.

There wouldn't be any problem walking as long as there was sidewalk, but soon she'd turn onto the country roads where she'd have to pick her way carefully in case there were patches of ice.

It wasn't dark, so that was good. She would have had to swallow her pride and ask Bill for help if it'd been dark. She remembered once when David had caught her walking home from Martha's in the dark. She'd stayed much longer than anticipated, and then had dallied along the way when she'd been distracted picking bouquets of wildflowers in a field not too far from Edmund's Pond. She kept envisioning how lovely the flowers would look on their table and on the dresser in their bedroom, and she'd spent much more time than she should have. When darkness began to fall, she'd increased her speed, but still she hadn't made it home before it grew pitch dark.

Within minutes, she'd heard a buggy coming toward her at a very slow speed. The lanterns hung in the front swung wildly and Leora noticed the driver was shining a flashlight onto the road, too. She realized it was David come to look for her. She stopped walking and waved her hands, which were full of flowers.

David drew up beside her and wasted no time in lecturing her about walking in the dark.

"But look, David," she'd said, "I've got beautiful flowers for the house."

He'd paused and stared at her. She saw the instant the anger and worry left him to be replaced with amusement.

"*Ach*, Leora," he'd said, groaning, "what am I to do with you? Get on in."

She'd scrambled into the buggy, and he'd kissed her soundly on the lips.

Now, Leora smiled in remembrance. It had been a sweet time together, and a lovely evening when they'd gotten home. She used to be more light-hearted. In fact, she remembered frequently teasing David and him laughing and even tickling her sometimes.

Well. Those days were long over. The responsibilities of the last year weighed heavily on her, and she feared that happy girl was gone forever. She stepped on a loose chunk of asphalt and nearly lost her balance. She righted herself and kept on, increasing her speed. *Englisch* people sometimes jogged this road. Leora had never jogged in her life. She wondered how it would feel to run a mile or more. If someone saw her, they'd think something drastic had happened. Her mind went to the fire at the Yoders and she shuddered. Better not think about that.

Leora guessed she'd been walking for close to an hour when she saw him coming. She knew it was Noah because she recognized Flicker. She slowed, wondering if he was coming for her. He stopped the buggy and called out to her.

"*Ach,* Leora! I'm so sorry. Come and get in."

She didn't argue. She crossed the street and climbed into the buggy, and the warmth inside made her eyes water.

"Can you ever forgive me? I didn't know when you'd be finished, but I figured I'd just go to the diner and wait for you. I was leaving the Feed & Supply when Eliza cornered me. I had to stock a top shelf before she'd let me leave. Are you frozen through and through?"

Leora looked into his worried face and felt herself relax. "*Nee,* Noah. I'm all right."

He kept looking at her, his gaze soft and full of regret. "I'm really sorry, Leora."

"Please don't worry about it," she said. But in truth, it felt nice to have someone worry about her.

"Let's get you home." He snapped the reins and turned his attention toward the road. He found a spot to turn around, and they were heading toward her house in no time.

She sank back into the seat and let the heat soak into her. In truth, it felt so warm and cozy in the buggy that she would have been happy to let Noah drive around for hours. Instead, he got her home in record time. She gazed at the outside of her little house, almost dreading to go in. She hadn't banked a fire, so it was going to be cold inside, and she hated to leave the warmth of the buggy. He pulled right up to her porch.

"Let me get your door," he said, and before she could protest, he'd run around the buggy to let her out.

She got out, once again plunged into the cold air.

"I'm going to grab an armful of wood and make sure your fire is going well," he told her. "Go on inside, and I'll be right in."

Her eyes widened. He hadn't even given her time to refuse his offer. He'd already disappeared around the side of her house, and she really wasn't inclined to stand there in the cold and wait for him. So, she did as she was bidden.

She unlocked her door and went inside. Even though it was still daytime, the inside of her house was fairly dark. The sky was overcast and not much light made its way through her windows. She quickly lit two lanterns, which bathed the cold room in plenty of light. Noah shoved through the front door, his arms full of chopped wood.

She hurried and closed the door behind him. He eyed the warming stove and made his way directly to it, letting the wood tumble out of his arms and into the metal box situated to the side of the stove.

"This should take you through the rest of the day and the night," he told her. Without preamble, he knelt before the stove and opened its iron door. He began placing wood inside, wadding up pieces of old newspaper she had saved for that very purpose.

She peeled off her cape and scarf and mittens, watching him. It was nice to have a man in her house, building a fire. She saw the look of concentration on his face and the way his shoulders moved beneath his heavy coat. His hat sat at the same jaunty angle as it always did, and she smiled. He really was a handsome man, and perhaps even more so when he was intent on something.

She realized what she was doing and gave a start. Standing about admiring Noah wasn't appropriate behavior for a widow of one year, was it? She shivered. And what if someone noticed his buggy in her drive and knew he was in there with her, alone? What might they think?

But still, him building her fire, making sure she was warm, was one of the nicest things anyone had done for her in a long time, and she simply couldn't believe that it was wrong.

"Would you like a cup of tea before you go?" she asked him.

He turned and she could see the surprised pleasure on his face.

"*Jah*," he told her. "That would be right nice."

"I'll get the kettle on." She quickly moved to the kitchen and set the kettle on the burner. She took out two cups and her jar of honey. She found her chamomile teabags and took two out.

She turned and nearly jumped. He was in the doorway, watching her.

"Oh," she said, flustered. "Is the fire going?"

"*Jah.* It's roaring now." He laughed. "It'll probably chase you out of the house before long."

She laughed with him. "The tea will be ready soon."

He looked around the kitchen and then came in and sat at her table. No man had sat at that table since she'd moved in. At that moment, Noah seemed larger than life, almost as if the kitchen weren't big enough to hold him. She swallowed and felt the dryness in her throat. She turned away, pretending to busy herself with the tea supplies, but in reality, she needed a minute to compose herself.

For a searing moment there, she'd been tempted to walk over to him and put her arms around him. She ached to hug someone and to be hugged in return. Her eyes burned. Until that moment, she hadn't realized just how lonely she truly was. She blinked rapidly and scolded herself for being so emotional.

The kettle whistled and she took it off the burner, pouring the steaming water into the waiting cups. She plopped a dollop of honey into each cup and then turned to Noah.

"Here you are," she said, serving him the tea.

She sat across from him, even though it meant squeezing in

against the wall. He must have noticed that she'd been eager to put space between them for his brow furrowed. The atmosphere became awkward, and she struggled to find something to say.

She took a sip of tea and so did he. Then he chuckled.

"What's so funny?" she asked.

"Us."

"What do you mean?"

"Sitting here like we've both gone mute."

She smiled. "You're right."

"Maybe we should spend a bit more time together. That way, we wouldn't feel so awkward."

Her brow rose. What was he suggesting? Was he wanting to court her? No. No. She was jumping to conclusions. Still, why would a single man want to be in the company of a widow?

"I see I've plunged us back into awkward," he said.

She blinked. She needed to answer him, but she suddenly couldn't speak. She needed to say no. It was too soon. *Too soon to even consider riding out with another man...*

When she didn't answer, his eyes took on a sad look. He took another drink of his tea. "I-I'll make it easy on you," he said, smiling sorrowfully. "I'll leave you alone now."

He stood and took his cup and saucer to the sink.

"You lock the door behind me, won't you?"

She got up quickly and followed him out to the front room. "Thank you for the ride home," she said.

"Anytime, Leora. And I mean that." He donned his hat, tipped his head in farewell, and was out the door.

She closed it and promptly locked it. Then she moved to the window and watched him get into his buggy and leave. She turned back to her front room, which suddenly seemed awfully empty. Almost cavernous, even though the room was not large.

She *should have answered him*. She touched her fingers to her lips. She'd wanted to say yes, and it had scared her. That was why she'd kept silent. Now, he was thinking she had no interest. It was too late now. She could hardly go chasing him down the road to tell him yes. Besides, she wasn't ready...

She swallowed hard and drew in a deep breath, wondering how to busy herself. Her chores were finished. She didn't bring any work home from the diner. She wasn't hungry. What should she do with herself?

She sank into her rocker and picked up her well-worn copy of *Little Women*. She tried to read it, but her mind kept wandering. She wondered what Martha was doing. Bustling about caring for the needs of her *kinner*, no doubt.

Leora glanced around her empty house.

Why couldn't she have *kinner* to care for? Would she ever?

And was she sure about what Noah had meant? She chewed the inside of her lip. She'd likely never know now. She was sure he'd taken her silence as a rejection.

She pressed a hand against her chest. But it hadn't been a rejection. He'd just taken her by surprise.

She found herself hoping he'd mention it again.

Chapter Twelve

Two nights later, Leora had fallen asleep in her rocker. She woke up to a cold room, the fire having gone completely out. Goodness, but she needed to get to bed. She went to the warming stove and opened the heavy door. She blew on the embers and there was a small spark. Perhaps she should throw another log in to warm up the house some.

But she decided against it. The warmth wouldn't reach her bedroom anyway. She turned down the wick of one of the lanterns, snuffing it out, and picked up the other to go to her room. It was then that she heard it. Sirens blasting somewhere in the area.

She stiffened. What was it? Usually, she couldn't hear any sirens unless they were going to someone's place in her district. She stopped moving and listened. Was it an ambulance? A police car? A fire truck?

She couldn't tell. A tremor of fear shot through her. Surely, it wasn't another fire. She sent up a quick prayer and hurried to the window, hoping to see something. But the siren was further away. She could see nothing. At times like that, she wished she had a phone. She wanted to know what was happening, but she could hardly get on her bicycle at that time of night and go pedaling madly down the road.

She set the lantern down and stared out the window, putting her arms around herself.

"*Gott*, take care of whoever it is or whatever it is..." she murmured.

She heard a second siren join the first, and she shuddered. Oh please, don't let it be someone hurt...

She didn't know what to do. But then, what could she do? The coldness of the room crept into her until she was shivering. She needed to get to bed; standing there in the cold wouldn't help anyone. Reluctantly, she picked up the lantern and went to her room. She quickly changed into her nightgown, went to the bathroom, and then returned and crawled into her cold bed. She should have heated a brick and put it between the sheets earlier.

Well, she hardly could have done that considering she'd fallen asleep in her chair. She lay on her side and pulled the quilts up to her chin, drawing her knees toward her chest. She closed her eyes, but she could still hear the sirens wailing. It was only one siren now, so she assumed that was a good sign.

She lay there with her eyes wide open. Sleep didn't seem within grasp. She tried to think of soothing things to relax herself, but it was of no use. And then she heard the gravel on her drive crunch and the sound of a horse snorting. She shot out of bed and ran through the dark to the front room. She peered out the window, expecting Martha's husband Tom again. But it wasn't Tom.

It was Noah.

She fumbled with the lock on the door and got it open right as he was about to knock.

"Noah!"

"I told Tom I'd check on you," he said. "It's another fire…"

"*Nee!*" she cried, covering her mouth with her hand.

"We think it's the same person or people that did this. It's the Gutzman's barn this time."

Marlie Gutzman had just given birth the week before. And wasn't her husband in Linder Creek for a few days to help his cousin?

"*Nee*," she said again. "Can I come and help? I could stay with Marlie."

"The men are all there helping. I-I don't know..."

"I'm coming," she insisted, dashing back to her bedroom. She lit her lantern and quickly got dressed. She bundled up and then ran into the kitchen and snatched up the fresh loaves of bread she'd made the day before. She doused the lantern and locked the door behind her.

"I don't know if I should—"

"I'm giving you no say in it, Noah. I'm going. I think Marlie's husband is away..."

"He is. Come on, then. She'll be glad to see you."

They hurriedly got into the buggy and were off. Again, Leora was grateful for Noah's buggy heater.

"Can they save any of the barn?"

"I don't know," Noah told her. "I hope so. The fire trucks got there sooner this time."

"And the animals."

"They're safe."

"Noah, who would do this? Who would do such a thing?"

She could see his grim face in the light from the streetlamp. "I don't know. It defies reason."

It defies reason. Yes. He was right. It did defy reason. They were silent then the rest of the way. When Noah turned into the

Gutzmans' place, it appeared to be in total chaos. But as she looked more closely, she saw a rhythm to the firemen's actions. The men from the district had saved some of the bales of hay, but they were now being held back by a fireman.

The blazes licked up the sides of the barn, and the whole yard was covered in a red glow. The sirens on top of the truck circled in a steady tempo. Water gushed from the hoses, forming arcs that could be mistaken for rainbows in a happier time.

And then Leora saw her. Marlie stood on the porch in her nightgown, her hands covering her face. Leora barely waited for Noah to stop the buggy before she jumped out and went racing across the lawn.

"Marlie," she cried. She went to her and held her with one arm, balancing the loaves of bread in her other. "Come on. Get inside. You'll catch your death out here."

"I c-can't. *Ach!* Leora! What will Bart say? He's out of town, you know. He's going to come back home to no barn. This is terrible! Leora, what am I going to do?"

"You're going to come inside," Leora said as softly as she could above the noise. "Come on."

She practically carried Marlie back into her house. Once inside, she saw the wide eyes of Marlie's oldest three. They were lined up on the couch, tears welling in their eyes.

"All right, *kinner*," Leora said, placing the loaves of bread onto a side table. "The firemen have everything well in hand. Your *mamm* just needs a minute to sit down, but you need to get back to bed now."

She spoke kindly and steadily as she helped Marlie into a chair and then went to shepherd the children upstairs.

"Who's going to show me which bed is which?" she asked, working to inject a playful note into her voice and grabbing a lantern. "Don't you fret. Tomorrow you'll be able to see the barn, and the animals are all safe, so no worries about that. Come on, now. Show me your beds."

She took them upstairs, had them all use the bathroom, and then followed them to their rooms. They didn't say much; although young Jake asked if he could help.

"You most certainly can," Leora told him. "But not till tomorrow. That's why you must get your sleep tonight."

She tucked them all in, kissed their foreheads, and walked back down the hallway to the stairs. Such sweet children. And the baby was sleeping through it all. Her heart ached for children of her own, but she didn't have time for such thinking right then. She had to tend to Marlie. When she got downstairs, Marlie was in the kitchen, making tea.

"I'm sorry," Marlie said, looking ashamed. "I kind of fell apart out there."

Leora glanced out the kitchen window. The lights on the firetruck were still circling but the flames had died down.

"At least the house is far enough away from the barn, that they weren't worried about us in here," Marlie went on. "I don't know what got into me. No lives were lost. I should be grateful." She looked over at Leora. "And I am. I am grateful."

"Of course, you are," Leora said gently. "But it's a shock, nevertheless. I think being a bit upset is nothing to be sorry about."

Marlie poured the hot water into a row of cups. "I thought the men might want some tea." She sighed and shook her head. "They're likely tired."

"They may want to just go home afterward," Leora said. "I can run out and ask them if you want me to."

"Would you?"

Leora nodded and then hurried outside, careful to stay out of the firemen's way. But they looked about finished with their job, and Leora breathed a sigh of relief. Noah saw her approach and went to her.

"Marlie has tea ready if anyone would like any."

"I'll tell the men," Noah said. "My guess is they'll just want to go home."

"I figured that. But anyway, would you offer it to them?"

"I will. And I'll be in later to give you a ride home."

"Thank you," she said, looking into his face smudged with soot. He was a good man, Noah King.

She was turning around when a policeman came over. "Were you here when it started?" he asked her.

"*Nee.* I came when it was well underway."

He looked toward the house. "Is the missus home? I understand her husband is gone."

"She's inside."

"I'll accompany you to the house then," he said and fell into step with her as they headed back inside.

Marlie gave a gasp when she saw him, and Leora quickly took off her cape and gave it to her so she could cover her nightgown.

"Excuse me, ma'am," the officer said. "I need to know if you saw or heard anything suspicious before the fire started."

Marlie's face turned white, and Leora feared she might fall over. She quickly stepped beside her and grabbed her arm.

"Marlie?" she asked softly. "Are you all right?"

Marlie squared her shoulders. "I did see something," she said, her voice shaking. "I was up because the *boppli* had fussed, but she fell back to sleep right away. I looked out my bedroom window and I saw..." She stopped and took a breath. "I thought I saw someone running away from the barn."

"Was it male or female?"

"I ... couldn't be sure. Male, I think. He was slight, you know, thin. He had on a sweatshirt or something with a hood. It was dark, so I couldn't see much."

The officer was busy taking notes. He looked up. "You couldn't see any hair color?"

"*Nee.* Not with the hood, and it was dark."

"What time was this?"

"Uh, I'm not certain. Just after midnight, maybe."

"Did you hear anything?"

"Not at first. But ... after the last fire, I was scared. I stared at the barn, praying, and then I saw it. The fire..."

"And?"

"I was afraid to go out there. I couldn't leave the *kinner* alone. I didn't know... I didn't know if he might come back..."

She was growing agitated, and Leora put her arm around her.

"It's all right, ma'am. I don't mean to upset you. You did real good. This information is helpful."

Leora could feel Marlie shudder against her.

"I-I don't have a phone," Marlie muttered. "I didn't know what to do. After a few minutes, I ran outside and saw that the fire was too big for me to put out. And then an *Englisch* person was driving by and must have seen it. They stopped and called it in on their phone. I-I didn't even get to thank them before they drove off."

She was crying now and Leora led her to a kitchen chair, and Marlie sank into it.

"Thank you again, ma'am. I may have more questions later, but I'll leave you for now." He closed his notebook and nodded, letting himself out.

Chapter Thirteen

Leora sat down next to Marlie. "I'm so sorry, Marlie."

"Will he be back?" she asked, grabbing Leora's arm. "Will the person come back and hurt the *kinner?*"

"I don't think so." Leora blew out her breath. "I don't think a person who starts a fire hurts people."

Marlie tensed. "Well, he's already hurt us!" she cried. "Look what he's done."

"That's not what I meant. And you're right. He's done enough damage."

"I'm not sure it was a man," Marlie said softly. "I think it was, but I'm not sure."

"The police will catch him," Leora said with a confidence she didn't feel.

"This is the *second* fire, Leora. They haven't caught him yet."

"I know."

They both grew silent and the graveness of the situation washed over them. And then Leora asked, "When does Bart get home?"

"Supposed to be in a few days, but I'll call the shanty close to his cousin's house. He'll come home right away."

"By tomorrow maybe?" Leora asked.

"If he gets the message soon enough," she said.

"*Gut.* That's *gut.*" She took Marlie's hand. "I'll stay with you tonight. Well, what's left of the night."

"*Ach,* you don't have to do that, Leora."

"I know I don't have to, but I'm going to." She stood. "I'm not sure the men will be in for tea. Why don't you go on up and go to bed? Then if the *kinner* wake, you'll hear them."

"They're scared, too."

"Probably. But they were tired. Hopefully, they're all fast asleep."

Marlie stood. "*Jah.* I should go up. The *boppli* might need fed soon anyway."

"Go on. I'll take care of things down here. Do you have a quilt? I can sleep on the couch."

"But that won't be comfortable."

"Of course, it will."

"There's a quilt in the sewing room," Marlie said.

"Then I'm set. Go on up."

Marlie gave her a quick hug. "Thank you, Leora."

"*Gut* night Marlie."

"*Gut* night."

Leora went to the window and looked out. It looked like the firemen were putting up their hoses. The police car was already gone, and most of the men from their district were also gone. She saw Noah see the last of them off and then he turned to the house. She went to the front door to let him in.

"The fire is out," he told her. He looked exhausted. His shoulders sagged, and he was covered with dirt and soot. "We were able to save a lot of the hay and some of Bart's equipment. I'm afraid he lost some of his plowing equipment, though. Maybe he can buy new with emergency funds from the district."

"I hope so."

"So here's another barn raising that'll be needed." He shook his head and gave a low whistle. "We're being targeted, Leora."

"I fear you're right."

He seemed to just notice that Marlie wasn't around. "Where's Marlie?"

"I sent her up to bed. I'm spending the rest of the night here."

"Then, I'm staying, too." He rubbed his forehead, smearing the soot. "I imagine Marlie is pretty shook up."

"She is." She touched his sleeve. "You don't have to stay, Noah."

"I reckon Marlie told you the same thing."

Leora laughed softly. "That she did."

"And it didn't do any *gut*, did it?"

"*Nee.*"

"So, you telling me the same thing ain't going to do any *gut* either. I'm staying. Let me see to my horse, and I'll be right back in."

"There's no barn for the horse."

"I know. I need to check on Marlie's animals, too. I'll see what I can do using the shed behind the house."

"Thank you," she murmured. He looked at her and something

passed between them. When he broke their gaze, she felt a surge of warmth toward him as he walked back outside.

She went to the warming stove and put in an extra log. Then she took the lantern and went into the sewing room. She saw a stack of quilts and took two, trying to find the most worn ones as poor Noah was mighty dirty. She didn't know if he'd want to shower in Marlie's bathroom or not. He might want to simply fall asleep in the rocker. David used to do that often enough.

She went back to the front room and sat on the couch waiting for him. He could be some time, if he was seeing to all the animals. But it wasn't long before he was back inside, rubbing his hands together.

"*Ach*, but it's cold out there behind the house. Someone already secured most of the animals. I'm not sure we corralled all the chickens. I'll check when it's light out again." He laughed. "Which won't be that long from now."

He gazed at her on the couch. "Go to sleep, Marlie. I'll just sit up in the chair here."

She smiled. "I brought a quilt in for you."

He looked down at himself. "I'm a mess. I don't want to dirty it." He peered about. Is there a bathroom downstairs? Or is the only one upstairs?"

"There's a bathroom off the kitchen. I don't think it has a shower, though."

"I can still wash my hands and face. I smell like a fire."

"Not surprising."

"Go to sleep. I'll wash up and tiptoe back in here." He smiled down at her and left the room.

She stifled a yawn. She was tired, but it was odd to go to sleep in the same room where Noah would be sitting. It felt funny to her. When he came back, she was still wide awake. He settled into the rocker next to the warming stove.

"You aren't asleep," he said quietly.

An air of intimacy filled the room, and she squirmed a bit, feeling even more uncomfortable.

"Marlie saw the person who started the fire."

Noah's eyes widened in the glow of the fire. "Did she?"

"It was someone wearing a sweatshirt with a hood."

"So she couldn't tell who it was."

"*Nee.* She didn't see his face. I don't think she would have recognized him anyway."

"Likely not."

"Noah?"

"Hmm?"

"Do you think he will come back?"

"*Nee*," he said quickly—almost too quickly. "I'm sure he won't. He's long gone."

"But won't he want to come back and see the damage?"

"I don't know, but it's too dark to see anything out there anyway. If he wants to see what he's done, he'd have to come in the daylight."

Leora shuddered.

"Please don't fret, Leora. I'm here. Everything will be all right. Go to sleep now."

His voice was soft and comforting and the more he spoke, the safer she felt. Her eyes grew heavy, and she thought she'd just close them for a little while. Not really go to sleep, just rest for a minute or two.

But it didn't go as planned, and she fell asleep almost immediately.

Chapter Fourteen

Noah rocked gently, staring at the fire through the small glass window in the warming stove's door. It was mesmerizing. He couldn't help but compare that contained flame to the raging inferno of the burning barn. Fire could be wonderful, or it could be disastrous. He stretched out his hands toward the stove, feeling the fire's warmth seep into his skin.

The flames danced and sputtered, and the room was pleasant even without the quilt. He turned his gaze to Leora who was now sleeping soundly. Her chest rose gently on each breath and her face looked so peaceful. Seeing her there like that, he realized that she often wore a pinched look, as if she were in a constant state of worry.

Was she? He wondered. Living alone, she would have a lot of responsibilities. And then, she had her job on top of that. The thought of Bill Jeffreys filled his mind. Was he pursuing Leora? Noah got the distinct impression that he was, and it rankled him. Bill Jeffreys had no business chasing after an Amish woman.

Noah wondered at the state of Leora's finances. She had to work, that was certain. But he wondered if she struggled from month to month. Most folks thought she'd sold her farm and bought the small house she lived in, but he knew better. Leora rented that house, which meant she hadn't made much of anything from the sale of her farm.

Had David Fisher been in debt? Noah frowned. If he had been, then Leora was carrying that worry, too.

She shifted slightly in her sleep and he watched her. He wanted to ease some of her burden; he wanted to see that look of peace on her face all the time. She was a good woman —special. He found himself yearning to be near her, even at the oddest times of day. In truth, if he had his way, he'd be with her all the time.

His face grew warm with the thought. He wanted to court her, but when he'd hinted at it the other day, he hadn't gotten the response he'd hoped for. Maybe it was too soon. She'd only been a widow a little over a year. And she had no children to support, so maybe she was in no hurry.

Would she ever be interested in another man? Or would she remain single as David's widow forever? The thought was distasteful, and he shoved it from his mind.

"Leora," he whispered. "Leora, you're a fine woman."

He drew in a long breath and closed his eyes. He could probably catch a few winks of sleep before it was time to get up.

Leora stirred and stretched. She opened her eyes and glanced around quickly, completely disoriented. And then she remembered. She was at Marlie's, and Noah...

Noah was gone. She sat up and stretched again. She needed to get breakfast started for everyone. She heard some stirring upstairs and figured that Marlie was likely with the baby. She folded the quilt and picked it up along with the one that Noah hadn't used and took them both back to the sewing room.

The kitchen was well-stocked. There was a bowl of eggs on the counter, probably gathered the day before. She set about making a large skillet full of scrambled eggs. She found some bacon in the refrigerator and put in on the griddle. She sliced up one of the loaves of bread she'd brought and placed the slices on a baking sheet to toast in the cook stove.

There was a distinct chill in the air, and she realized she hadn't built up the fire. Well, she'd get to that after the eggs were cooked. The side door opened and a whoosh of cold air swept through the house.

"*Gut* morning," Noah greeted her, coming into the kitchen.

"*Gut* morning, Noah," she returned the greeting. "I'll have breakfast on the table right quick."

He grinned. "Sounds fine. I'll stir up the fire in a minute. I've checked on the animals and managed to find a few more chickens."

"I imagine they weren't too happy," she commented.

He laughed. "*Nee.*" He strode to the kitchen window over the sink and peered out. "It's a right mess out there."

She joined him at the window. "It breaks my heart."

"They'll find him," Noah said.

"But when? And is someone else's barn in danger tonight? And what if he starts in on Amish homes?"

He put his hand on her arm and she felt his touch to her very core. "Don't think such things, Leora. That won't happen. We're all praying."

She shook her head. "Right. Of course, you're right. *Gott* is watching over us."

"He is," Noah said softly.

"*Ach*, Noah!" Marlie cried, entering the kitchen with her baby on her hip. "When did you get here?"

"He never left," Leora told her.

"You spent the night?"

Noah nodded. "I did. I figured it wouldn't hurt to have a man around."

Marlie's eyes filled with tears. "You're both so kind. Thank you." She shifted the baby from one hip to the other. "I need to get to the shanty and leave a message for Bart."

"I can do that for you," Noah said. "Just give me the number."

"It's written on the notepad right over there," Marlie said, indicating the pad with a nod of her head. She bit her lip. "Have you looked at the damage?" she asked, her voice faltering.

"Your barn is gone," Leora told her softly. "Completely gone."

Marlie sucked in a breath, and Leora could see her gather her courage to approach the window. She moved slowly to the sink and looked outside. She made a small gasp and covered her mouth with her free hand.

"It can be rebuilt," Noah said, his voice gentle. "You let the district worry about that."

Marlie shook her head over and over and didn't say a word. Then she looked at Noah. "And the animals? They're still all right?"

"They're fine. I've already been out to check on them. I put some of them in the shed. I can clear out more of the shed to have room for a few others tonight. The chickens are mostly gathered now. But I'll have to fix the coop."

"But you have your own work..." Marlie said.

"That I do. But I'm glad to help. Bart will be back soon, but there are things I can do before he arrives. Right now, I'll get the fire going. There's a bit of a chill in here."

Tears were slipping down Marlie's cheeks now. "Thank you," she eked out.

"Breakfast is about ready," Leora announced, putting some brightness in her tone. "Shall I wake the *kinner*?"

Marlie blinked and sniffed. "I'll get them." She walked to Leora and grabbed her hand. "Thank you," she murmured and then left the room to fetch the children.

Noah returned to the kitchen as the eggs finished cooking so Leora scooped them into a bowl. "I need to set the table," she said, looking for the plates in the cupboard.

"Let me help," Noah told her. "I'm not entirely useless in the kitchen."

She smiled at him with gratitude. "All right, then. You can prove it to me."

He laughed and tweaked the string of her *kapp* before reaching past her into the cupboard.

Chapter Fifteen

Marlie's *kinner* were solemn during breakfast. Noah had eaten quickly and gone to the shanty to make a call to Linder Creek. Leora bustled about cleaning up the dishes and putting the butter and jam away.

"Hopefully, Bart will get the message right away," Marlie said. "If someone else checks the phone shanty, they'll likely tell Bart's cousin there's a message for him."

"I have a feeling he'll be here by tonight, Marlie." Leora picked up the pitcher of milk. "I can stay the day if you like."

"You've already done so much. I'm sure you're needing to get home," she said, adding, "to your chickens, at least."

Leora smiled. "They can peck at the ground till I get there. But you're right. Shall I come over later?"

Marlie shook her head. "I imagine I'll have visitors today."

"If Bart doesn't come home today, I'll stay the night again."

"Leora, *nee*. You've done enough."

Leora shook her head. "I don't mind, Marlie. Truly, I don't."

Marlie bit her lip. "All right. If Bart isn't home, I'd appreciate you staying."

Leora took the milk and put it in the refrigerator. Just then, Noah returned. "Message delivered," he told Marlie.

"Thank you, Noah."

Noah turned to Leora. "Are you ready to go home?"

She nodded. "But if Bart doesn't arrive today, I'll be returning for the night again."

Noah nodded. "I think that's a *gut* idea. Marlie, I'll come by this afternoon to clear out the shed and see to your animals. You should know by then if Bart is coming. If not, I'll swing by and get Leora and bring her over."

"Thank you," Marlie said once again.

"Give me a minute to get the buggy hitched," Noah told Leora. "Then come on out, and I'll take you home."

He winked at Marlie's children and then went back outside. Marlie looked at Leora. "Well?" she asked.

"Well, what?"

"Are you and Noah courting?" Marlie had lowered her voice. Then she smiled. "I don't know why I'm whispering. It's not like my *kinner* are going to rush about with the news."

Leora had a sudden wish that they were courting, but she pressed it down. It was too early yet. She needed to grieve David's passing longer, didn't she? And the holidays were coming. Thanksgiving had almost arrived. She knew the holidays were going to be hard for her without him, and she wasn't of a mind to have anyone close enough to see her pain.

"*Nee*," she said. "Noah is just helping me with transportation since I don't have a buggy, and it's getting right cold for my bicycle."

Marlie frowned. "Why did you sell your buggy? Didn't you and David have a nice one?"

Leora shrugged, trying to look nonchalant. "We did, but at the time, I thought my bicycle was sufficient." *And I needed the money.*

"You could get a new one," Marlie suggested. "And isn't there an outbuilding behind your house where you could stable a horse?"

"I'll think on it," Leora said, hoping to bring the discussion to an end.

"I think Pete Miller has a pony for sale."

Leora stifled a sigh. "Thank you, Marlie," she said, forcing a smile. "I'll keep that in mind."

"I just don't like the idea of you freezing every time you go anywhere," Marlie continued.

"I think Noah will be ready for me now," Leora interrupted, putting on her cape and mittens and scarf. "Maybe I'll see you this evening."

"Thank you for everything."

"You're more than welcome," Leora said. She walked to where Marlie's children were splayed on the large rag rug, playing. She bent over and tousled their hair. "Bye, *kinner*. You be *gut* for your *mamm*."

They grinned up at her, and she left to their waves of farewell.

Noah was just bringing the buggy around. She wasted no time in getting in.

"Marlie really appreciated you staying the night," he told her.

"And you, too."

He tipped his head. "I was glad to do it." He frowned. "I'm not really excited about you being alone these nights."

"I'll be fine." She folded her hands in her lap. "I'm used to it, and I'm locking my doors. And I don't have a barn, remember?"

"You have that building out back."

"It wouldn't be a very exciting fire," she said, trying to inject some levity into the conversation, but it didn't work. It didn't work at all.

Noah looked at her. "It's not a joking matter."

"I know. Sorry."

"I like the idea of you staying with Marlie."

"I'll be happy to if Bart doesn't return."

"And I'll stay again, too."

Leora was surprised at that. She understood him staying with them the night of the fire, but how would it look if he camped out there again with her and Marlie? She scowled, disgusted with herself. Sometimes public appearances weren't that important, were they? She nearly scoffed out loud. Of course, they were. Public appearances were of utmost concern in their district.

Still, she couldn't control what Noah did, and she quite liked the thought of his presence during the night. She shuddered. What would she do if she saw a hooded person lurking around? Would she have the nerve to leave her house and try to make it to the phone shanty? What if it was pitch dark? Would she go then?

"What are you thinking?" Noah asked, studying her face as he gently snapped the reins.

"Um, nothing."

"Are you worried?"

"I was thinking about what I'd do if I saw the hooded person."

He grimaced. "Pray," he said. "The whole district should be praying right now."

"I'm sure everybody is. Do you think the bishop will call a special prayer meeting?"

"It wouldn't surprise me. If he does and if you want to go, I can take you."

"Thank you," she murmured.

When he turned into her drive, she could feel him studying her again. "You're sure you're all right here by yourself?"

"Of course, Noah. I'm fine. It's my home."

"If you need anything, I'll be at my farm until mid-afternoon, then I'll check on Marlie."

"All right. Thank you." She gave him a smile before slipping out of the buggy. She hurried up her steps and unlocked her door, going inside. Only after she shut the door again and locked it did she hear Noah take off.

What a night they'd had. She was tired and felt grungy, but she needed to see to her chickens first. Then she'd shower and maybe bake something for Marlie's family. She went out the side door and scattered seed for her chickens. They fluttered and pecked happily, seeming no worse for having to wait a bit longer for breakfast. Outside, Leora glanced around more carefully than usual. She realized that she was looking for the hooded person.

She laughed. How unlikely that whoever it was would be lurking around her house. In fact, her house didn't look so obviously Amish. She had no barn, no buggy sitting around, no horse or cow grazing out back. She gazed at her house. But there were no electrical wires running to the house, and there was the clothesline which was completely visible from the street.

Her house looked Amish all right.

Sighing, she went back inside, locking the side door behind her. She was walking toward her bathroom when she heard the crunch of gravel from out front. Was Noah back? Had he forgotten to tell her something?

She went to the front room window and peered out. It wasn't a buggy at all. It was Bill Jeffreys's truck. She sucked in her breath and her hands quickly went to her hair. She patted it, making sure it was still tucked neatly under her *kapp*. She opened the front door and stepped outside.

He was getting out of his truck. "Oh Leora," he called. "I heard about the fire. That's two in one week."

He shut his cab door and came to her, climbing the steps of her porch. "Are you all right?"

"I'm fine, Bill. Truly." Her breath made wispy puffs of steam in the cold air.

"I left Donna at the grill. The woman hates me now." He laughed. "But as soon as I heard, I had to come check on you."

"I appreciate it. But I'm fine."

He smiled down at her, and she warmed at his concern.

She hesitated, debating a bit before saying, "Can you come in for a minute? Would you like some tea?"

He nodded and she could see how pleased he was. "I can stay for a while. Not too long, though, or my sister might plan my demise." He laughed again and followed her inside the house.

She went to the kitchen and put the kettle on. She could do with some tea, too. When she returned to the front room, she saw Bill kneeling before the warming stove, coaxing a fire to life. She smiled. He looked natural there, blowing into the stove and feeding it kindling. The fact that he'd thought to get the fire going surprised her. For some reason, she didn't think of the *Englisch* as having fire-building skills—an unfair generalization, she supposed.

"Thank you," she said.

He glanced over at her. "I can't have my best employee freezing to death, now can I?"

She smiled. "I don't imagine I'd freeze."

"I've got it going now," he said with satisfaction. He put in another log and then stared at the flames a while longer before closing and latching the door. "I assume you knew the family whose barn was burnt."

"*Jah*. I spent the night over there."

He stood. "You did? You must be exhausted then."

"I am somewhat. In truth, I just got home."

His brow furrowed. "Oh dear. And then you have company within the first minute or two. You probably want to lie down for a bit. I won't stay…"

"The tea is almost ready. Surely, you can stay long enough to drink a cup." Why in the world was she pushing him to stay? He was right. She was exhausted. Yet, looking at him, seeing his concern for her, touched her and made her wish he would stay—if only for a while.

"I suppose I could have a bit." He laughed. "Or as those in England say, a spot of tea." He'd put on an accent, and she laughed. It felt good to laugh, and she realized just how tense she was.

He followed her into the kitchen and sat at her table. How odd. No man had ever sat there until just recently, and now two different men had been there within days of each other. Bill Jeffreys wasn't a big man, not as big as Noah, but he still filled the room. She poured the tea, thinking how nice it was to have two kind men in her life.

And just that quickly, shame filled her. What was she doing? Was she encouraging these men somehow? Did they both have intentions toward her?

Was she betraying David's memory?

"We just got a huge reservation for Thanksgiving dinner," Bill said. "A party of eighteen want to have their meal at the diner."

Leora gave a start, yanked from her ruminations. "*Ach*, but that's *gut, ain't so?*"

"Sure is. And we always have others who come by. We may have to add a couple extra tables for the day. Donna is pleased."

"I'm glad." She served him the tea and then stood by the counter, sipping hers.

"You're not going to join me at the table?" he asked, his voice thick.

She licked her lips, feeling suddenly awkward. For a quick moment, she wished it were Noah sitting there. He was Amish, and this man wasn't. She couldn't forget that.

"I-I could join you," she said, sitting at the end of the table.

He reached over and put his hand over hers. She felt his warmth sink into her.

"I'm real sorry about what's happening right now to your people. Are you scared?"

His frankness disconcerted her. "I, uh, well, it is a bit of a worry."

"You're likely wondering who will be next."

She stared at him. Was he reading her mind now?

He sighed. "I would be wondering if I were you. Do the police have any leads? Have they made any progress at all?"

She shrugged. "Not that I know of."

"I'm glad you don't have a barn, Leora." He squeezed her hand and then removed his. She stared down at where his fingers had been. She blinked hard and then took a sip of the hot tea.

"How did you get home this morning? Please don't tell me that you rode your bike."

"*Nee*," she said, shaking her head. "I didn't ride my bicycle."

He gave her an expectant look and waited.

"Noah gave me a ride home," she said, wondering why she felt like keeping it a secret. What difference would it make to Bill Jeffreys?

But it did make a difference. She could see it in his eyes.

"I see," he said. Silence stretched out between them, until he asked, "So. Is he your boyfriend?"

"Noah?" she asked, although she knew full well he meant Noah.

"Yes. Noah."

Bill's sister had asked her the very same thing the other week. She gave Bill the same answer. "*Nee,* he's not."

Bill's shoulders relaxed, but Leora felt uneasy. Noah wasn't her beau, but many times lately, it seemed as though he was. By saying no, it almost felt as if she were betraying him—the same way it felt as though she were betraying David.

Suddenly, she was exhausted. Tired to her very bones. She put her cup down. Bill was watching her closely.

"I think I better go," he said, standing. "Thank you for the tea, Leora."

She scrambled up from the table, too. "You're welcome."

"Don't come in today, all right. You stay home and rest." He looked down at her with tenderness. "Take care of yourself."

"I-I will," she whispered.

"Don't see me out. I know my way." He gave her a winning smile and was gone.

She sank back onto her chair and stared at her cooling cup of tea. She needed to go to bed. Maybe she would sleep for days. She didn't like all the confusion whirling inside her. And the fear. Not until this last week had she felt afraid to stay alone.

She had felt lonely and sad, even a bit displaced, but never so afraid.

She didn't like it. With an impatient sigh, she carried both cups to the sink. The house was warming up nicely now; Bill must have made a good fire. It'd burn for a while without her interference. She should take a shower, but she didn't.

Instead, she walked straight to her bedroom, fell onto the bed, pulled a quilt over herself without even changing her clothes, and went straight to sleep.

Chapter Sixteen

It wasn't but two hours later, that something awakened Leora. She opened her eyes and tried to orient herself. What was that? It was a scraping noise of some kind. Instant fear grabbed her, and she jolted upright in bed. There it was again. She tossed off the quilt and got up. She went to her window and forced herself to look outside. It was overcast and the clouds hung low, as if they were ready to dump snow. The fields behind her house stretched bleakly across the land. There was nothing out of the ordinary.

She didn't move. Only listened.

Nothing.

But there had been something. She'd heard it clearly. Her chickens didn't seem to be disturbed because she heard nothing from them. If it was a critter out there, they'd be squawking and having a fit. She left her bedroom and went to the kitchen. The sound had seemed to come from the side of the house. She couldn't get a good view of the side of the house from the kitchen, but she went to window anyway and looked outside. Again, nothing.

She shivered and then scolded herself. It was the middle of the day, and there she was hovering about as if she were under attack or something. This was ridiculous. There could be nothing to hurt her at this hour of the day.

Aggravated with herself, she tried to ignore the situation, but she couldn't. Finally, with a sigh, she put on her cape and slipped her heavy black shoes back on. She didn't need to get dressed as she hadn't undressed. Her feeling of grunginess from that morning had only increased. She would for sure clean up after she had a look around outside.

She unlocked the side door and stepped into the cold. She could see the chicken coop now, and nothing was out of order. She glanced over to her shed and noticed that the door was ajar. Now, that was odd. She never left it open, but then, the latch was old, and it could have opened on its own, she supposed.

In truth, she didn't believe that, but she held onto the thought anyway. Anything else was likely to only increase her feeling of uneasiness. She walked slowly toward the shed, half expecting a hooded person to jump out and attack her. She swallowed and kept walking. When she got to the shed, she pulled the door open. It had a loose dirt floor and she clearly saw footprints right inside the door.

She gave a snort. Well, of course she'd see footprints. She was going in and out of the shed all the time to get chicken feed and her bike and tools when she needed them. Still, she couldn't help but study the prints more closely. Her breath caught and she leaned close to the ground.

There was the definite imprint of a large shoe, much larger than hers. To make sure she wasn't fooling herself, she stepped into the print. Her shoe didn't come close to filling it. She jerked upright and stepped back, her breath coming fast. Had someone been in there? And why?

She glanced around the shadowed insides, looking for smoke. She inhaled deeply. There was no smell of fire.

Ach, but she was being foolish. There had to be an explanation for the footprint. Then she remembered that Noah had come out for firewood just the other day. The footprint could easily have been his. She leaned heavily on the door. She didn't keep any firewood in the shed. It was kept under the large overhanging eave toward the back of the house, easily visible. There would have been no reason for him to enter the shed.

Her heart was beating wildly now, and despite the freezing air, sweat broke out on her upper lip. Who had been here? And since she'd just heard the noise, were they still around?

Were they inside the shed, lurking behind something?

In panic, she slammed the door shut and closed the latch and ran back inside her house, locking her side door with fumbling fingers. She stumbled to the kitchen table and sank down on her chair.

No. No. No. She was being ridiculous. *Ach,* but those fires had gotten inside her brain. There was a perfectly good explanation for both the noise and the footprint—she just didn't know it. Her imagination was playing tricks on her. Goodness, but she'd have a good laugh about this later. Why, she could even tell Noah about it, and they'd laugh together.

Noah. She wished he were there. She glanced out the kitchen window as if wishing would conjure him up. But all she saw were the naked branches of her oak tree reaching to the sky like a massive disjointed rake, rustling ever so slightly in the breeze.

Her heart was beating wildly, and she worked to take slow calm breaths.

She was being ridiculous.

Where was Noah? Why didn't he come?

Why should he? she asked herself. He had no cause to come over right then. She needed to stop shivering. *Do something,* she told herself. *Get up and do something.*

She stood up and looked around almost frantically. No dirty dishes to wash. Wait. She hadn't eaten for a while. She could fix herself a nice meal. That would be calming. And she could pray while she worked. Yes. This was a good idea.

She murmured a prayer to God as she went about fixing herself a nice fat sandwich of left-over meatloaf. She was generous with the ketchup and mustard, slicing the sandwich into neat halves. She poured a glass of milk and sat down to eat. She said another silent prayer and then picked up one of the halves and took a bite.

It was good. In truth, the meatloaf had been one of her best. But right then, she could hardly enjoy it. Her gaze kept darting outside, scanning her yard. Was he there? The hooded man? Was he somehow watching her right then? She jolted from her chair and yanked the curtains closed. She swallowed hard and sat back down.

She picked up her sandwich and took another bite, but she couldn't do it. She couldn't eat. She forced herself to chew and swallow the bite and then dropped the sandwich back to the plate.

What was wrong with her? This wasn't like her. She wasn't a fearful person. She stood up and began pacing a circle in her small kitchen. This was unacceptable. She would not live like this.

Goodness, but she hadn't even taken off her cape. Good. She would go back outside. Prove to herself that she was being ridiculous. Prove to herself that she wasn't a fearful woman who cowered inside at the merest breath of danger.

She would go out the front door this time. She would go out there for anyone to see. And she would check on her chickens, and she would go to the shed, open it up, and grab a few handfuls of seed. The chickens wouldn't mind being fed another time that day. Maybe they'd reward her with a couple extra eggs the next morning.

She smiled at the thought and went outside, stepping bolding onto the front porch as if proclaiming her presence to the world. Then she marched around the house to the shed and clenching her jaw, she slid open the latch. She opened the door, letting the light fall in a swath of white onto the dirt floor. She stepped inside, reaching into the feed bag. She took two handfuls of seed and went to the coop, deliberately leaving the shed door open to prove to herself that she wasn't afraid.

She scattered the seed, to the delight of her chickens. They fluttered about, pecking the earth with complete cackling joy. She grinned at their display of enthusiasm. The cold nipped at her cheeks, and she began to feel some better. Nothing like watching chickens to lighten one's spirits. When her fingers began to grow numb, she turned back to the shed to go over and close it.

It was closed. She gasped and froze, and the truth slammed into her. There had been someone inside. She had trapped someone and then let them free. She swallowed and her chest tightened. Wait. Maybe the wind had closed the door. She was creating scenarios again. Imagining things. She swallowed and walked the short distance to the shed, biting her lower lip to keep it from trembling.

The shed door was latched.

She fell back a step. She was *not* imagining things. The wind had *not* shut the door. Tears sprang to her eyes and for a long minute, she couldn't move. The cold air filled her, and she shivered.

Go inside. Go inside. Go inside.

She hadn't locked the front door. What if whoever it was had gone into her house? No. They wouldn't have. This behavior made no sense, right? The hooded man was an arsonist, not a murderer.

Murderer?

Her mind was going crazy now. Without thinking, she went to her shed, opened the door again and rolled out her bicycle. After latching the door, she mounted her bicycle and took off down the road. She was so intent on her mission that she barely felt the frigid breeze that blew against her.

She wanted to go see Noah. He'd know what to do. But she could hardly do that, could she? A widow pedaling over to a single man's farm? She couldn't do that. She'd go to Martha's. It was only a bit further down the road. She'd feel better if she stayed a while at Martha's house. Besides, hadn't she promised Martha she would visit more often?

And if Tom were there, he could come back with her and check her house for intruders.

She heard a car behind her and moved as far to the side of the road as she could. It zoomed past, its tailwind making her waver slightly. She was becoming more aware of the cold air, but she ignored it. Martha's house wasn't that far away.

But when she neared Noah's house, which came first, she couldn't help herself. She turned in and rode straight to the barn. The door was open, and she felt sure Noah would be inside. He saw her coming before she spotted him.

"Leora!" he called.

She looked to where his voice came from and saw him put down some kind of tool. He walked straight to where she'd stopped, straddling her bike. His brow furrowed.

"What is it? You look spooked." He grabbed her arm. "What's happened?"

"I-I..." And suddenly, she couldn't speak further. She began to cry and then was so ashamed of herself that she sputtered, trying to hide it. "I-I'm fine. It's just that ... that..."

He held onto the handle of her bike. "Get off, Leora. Take a breath. Climb off. There you go."

He set her bicycle on the ground and turned to her. "What's happened?"

She looked up at him, at the concern in his eyes, and began to cry all over again. He put his arm around her shoulder and drew her inside the barn out of the breeze.

"Are you hurt?"

She shook her head, sniffling and wiping at her eyes. "I-I'm sorry."

"For what? You've nothing to be sorry for. *Ach*, you're cold, Leora. Let's go inside."

She shook her head. She couldn't go inside his house. What would people think?

"Come on," he said. His arm was still around her shoulder and despite her protests, he took her straight into his house. "Sit down," he instructed, leading her to the rocker beside his warming stove. He knelt before the stove, poked around inside a bit and put in another log. Closing the door, he got up and pulled another rocker close to hers. He sat down.

"Take your time," he said. "But I want to know what happened."

Chapter Seventeen

Leora pressed a hand against her chest, and her breathing slowed. She felt absurd now, sitting there, like a hysterical woman. She took another breath. "I'm sorry. It's n-nothing."

"Clearly, it's not nothing if you're upset."

"I think... I think that the hooded person was in my shed," she told him.

He jumped out of his chair. "*What?* Did you see him?"

Her eyes widened. She hadn't expected such a reaction from him.

He leaned close. "Did you see him? Did he hurt you?" His voice rose with every word.

"*Nee*," she said. "*Nee*. I didn't see him. But I saw his footprints, and he closed and latched my shed while I was feeding my chickens."

Noah was staring at her now, his expression hard and alarmed. "You're sure?"

She nodded. "And I didn't... Well, I didn't lock my front door when I went out this time and I was..." Could she admit it to him? Could she admit her fear? But he already knew, didn't he? She was there, wasn't she? "I was afraid he had gone into my house."

Noah hands fisted at his sides. "You didn't go in, did you?"

"*Nee.* I'm sorry. I should have checked..."

"*Nee,* you shouldn't have. You did the right thing. I'll go back there. I'll check inside."

"But what if... What if he's dangerous?"

"He sets fires, Leora. I'll be all right. You can stay here and wait till I get back."

"*Nee!*" she cried, and then felt embarrassed at the frantic note in her voice. "I want to go with you."

He studied her for a long moment. "All right. We'll go together. I'll put your bicycle in the back of my buggy."

She let out her breath, not realizing she'd been holding it. "Thank you, Noah."

He touched her cheek with the back of his fingers. She felt

his rough skin, felt the warmth of his hand, felt the emotion of his touch, and her eyes burned with unshed tears.

"Thank you for coming to me..." he said softly.

"I wasn't going to," she whispered. "I was really heading for Martha's house."

He smiled tenderly at her. "But you didn't make it there."

She shook her head. "I didn't make it there..."

"I'm glad. I'll hitch up the buggy, and we'll go."

She helped him hitch up Flicker, and he smiled at her more than once over the horse's back. He hefted her bicycle into the back of the buggy and they both got in. Neither said anything as they drove to her house. She glanced at him every few moments and saw the set of his jaw and the look of determination on his face.

"Do you... Do you think we should contact the *Englisch* police?" she asked.

He shook his head. "At this point, there's no need. We don't know for sure if he's even still there."

"Maybe I imagined it all," she said, now that her nerves had settled some. "Maybe it was all in my mind."

He looked at her. "I don't think you would have imagined a shed door shut and latched," he said. "Nor would you have imagined footprints in the dirt."

She swallowed and nodded. He believed her. He didn't think she was being emotional.

It didn't take long to arrive at her house. Noah drove the buggy straight to the porch and got out. He paused before shutting the buggy door.

"I'd rather you stay here," he said.

She didn't argue, she just nodded.

He shut the buggy door and climbed her porch steps and disappeared inside. Leora didn't know what she expected, but she scooted forward on her seat and every muscle in her body was tense. She was waiting to hear him holler or to hear footsteps fleeing the scene or something.

But all was quiet. She held her breath, her eyes glued to the front door of her house.

And then Noah appeared again. He shut her door and came down to the buggy. He spoke through the buggy window. "If he was here, he's gone now."

She let out her breath in a whoosh.

"Will you show me the footprints?"

She swallowed and got out of the buggy, leading him around to her shed. She opened the door and looked down. She'd forgotten that she'd come in after she saw the footprints, and they were all but obscured completely beneath her own prints.

"I'm sorry," she said. "I came in here afterward. They were right there." She pointed to the ground.

He squatted and studied the dirt. "I can kind of see where there might have been a large print." He stood up then and went further inside the shed. She stayed at the door, watching him look around. He peered behind the bags of feed and also pulled a few pieces of stored plywood away from the back wall.

"He could have hidden back here," he said.

She shuddered. "*Jah*. That's what I had thought."

"The shed doesn't lock?"

"Just the latch on the outside."

He rubbed his chin. "I think I'll put a padlock on the door."

"Is that really necessary?" she asked. She had mixed feelings about that—part of her saw the value and liked the idea, but she hated to put Noah to the trouble. And she didn't like the fact that the hooded man—if that's who was there—was controlling them in a way.

"*Jah*. If not for you, for me." He came out of the shed and gazed down at her. "I will worry about you, Leora."

She blinked and felt her throat tighten.

"What do you think about staying with Martha for a few

days? I'm sure she'd welcome you. At least until the person is found."

"But what if he's never found? I'm going to have to live here by myself again anyway."

"That is true. But maybe, he'll be caught soon. Then the danger will be over."

She squared her shoulders. She couldn't bear to be that fearful woman. "*Nee.* I'm staying here. I'll be fine, Noah. It's just that I forgot to lock the door. I won't forget anymore."

"Leora, please..."

"*Nee.* I will stay here, but I'll be more careful. I promise."

"I just don't like it."

She smiled at him, pulling forth all her courage. "I know you don't. But truly, Noah, I'll be fine."

"Isn't there someone you'd like to invite here to stay, then?"

She laughed softly. "*Nee.* I'm all right."

He blew out his breath.

"Thank you, though. For bringing me home and checking my house. I appreciate it." She suddenly became aware of the fact that she hadn't washed or freshened up since yesterday morning. She took a step back, wondering just how bad she looked.

"I will come over anytime you need me," he told her. "Don't hesitate to come find me."

"I won't," she said, knowing she would. How could she be bothering him all the time? It wasn't seemly.

"Thank you again, Noah."

"You're not going in to work, are you?" he asked.

"*Nee.* Not today."

"Do you need a ride tomorrow?"

"Um... I don't know yet."

"I'll stop over in the morning and check. Is that all right?"

She smiled again. Goodness, but this man made her smile continually. "That would be fine."

He still seemed hesitant to go, but he finally walked back to his buggy. She went around to her porch and waved him off. And then she went inside. She carefully locked the door behind her. She would take a shower immediately this time. And put on a new frock.

Then she remembered that she'd left her partially eaten meatloaf sandwich out on the table. She went to the kitchen and saw it sitting there. Her first thought was that Noah had seen it. What would he think about her leaving half-eaten food around? She was becoming more and more vested in what Noah thought, but *ach*, he was such a nice man.

She liked him. Perhaps, more than liked him. She picked up her sandwich, noting that the bread was now dry. She didn't want it; although, she was hungry. She hated to waste food, but in this case, she was going to. She dumped the sandwich into the garbage can. The glass of milk she'd poured had gone warm. She poured it into a saucepan, deciding that a hot cup of cocoa would do nicely right then.

She laughed when she'd fixed it and sat down to drink. Once again, she'd put off her shower.

Chapter Eighteen

Noah was troubled. He didn't like the fact that Leora insisted on staying alone. When he went later that afternoon to Marlie's place, he couldn't shake the feeling that something was going to happen to Leora.

Marlie came right out to the front porch when he arrived.

"Thank you, Noah," she called out. "Bart is coming home. He should be here any minute. He found a van driver right away."

"That's *gut* news," Noah answered. He secured the reins and got out of the buggy. "How are you doing?"

"I'm doing fine," she said. And indeed, she looked much better this time. "People have been by. The bishop came, too. He's calling a special prayer meeting at five o'clock today—at his place."

"*Gut.* Will you go? And Bart will be back in time, right?"

"Surely, he will," she said. "And we'll go. We need to pray not only for safety but for the person responsible. He must be filled with hate."

Noah wondered. What was it that made a person do such things? He thought it was more likely fear than hate. Fear of the unknown. Fear of something different.

"I want to thank you again for last night," Marlie told him.

"Nothing to thank me for," he said, and he meant it. He could list a dozen men who would have done the same thing without a second thought.

"And Leora. You were both so *gut* to me."

The sound of a baby crying reached his ears.

"*Ach,* that's the *boppli.* I need to go. Would you like to come in for a bite?" Marlie asked.

"*Nee.* I'm fine. I just wanted to make sure all was well."

"As well as can be expected."

"How was Bart doing when you talked to him?"

"He was mostly worried about me and the *kinner.* Of course, he's upset, but he was praising the *gut* Lord that we're all safe. 'A barn can be rebuilt' he told me."

"He's right."

The *boppli's* cries increased.

"I do need to go now."

"Of course. I'll be seeing you at the prayer meeting."

"*Jah*. Bye, Noah."

"Bye."

Noah got back in his buggy. As he drove by the burnt remains of the barn, his mind returned to thoughts of Leora. He was fairly certain she'd want to go to the prayer meeting. She would probably need a ride, too, unless someone else went by to fetch her.

His thoughts immediately switched to Bill Jeffreys, and he shook his head, huffing out his breath. It wasn't likely that Bill Jeffreys would even know about the prayer meeting, much less give Leora a ride to it. Goodness...

Plain and simple, Noah was jealous of Bill Jeffreys.

Ach, but he needed to get control of himself.

He drove back to his farm, still shaking his head.

Leora wished she'd agreed to go in to work that day. It would have given her something else to think about. As it was, her mind kept circling and circling the hooded stranger. Every five minutes, she was craning her neck, looking outside, expecting to see the person gaping in at her. She tried cleaning her house—which barely took half an hour. She tried baking—it was the worst loaves of bread she produced in years. She tried reading—but her eyes simply skimmed the words without paying a stick of attention.

Then she set to pacing. Well, at least she'd get a bit of exercise.

Near supper time, she nearly wept with relief when she heard a buggy come into her drive. She hurried to the front door, unlocked it, and opened it.

Tom pulled to a stop in front of the porch. Martha climbed out. She was waddling a bit this time, and Leora couldn't help but smile.

"Leora, you coming to the prayer meeting?"

"What prayer meeting?"

"The bishop called it. We're going to pray about these fires. The meeting is at his place."

"*Jah.* I'll come," Leora said. "Let me get my cape."

She hurried back inside, grateful to have something to do. It was good of Tom and Martha to come by for her. She took a moment to bank the fire, and then she grabbed her cape. She glanced around the room. It'd be dark by the time she got back, and she didn't fancy coming into a dark house. Not today. But leaving a lantern burning unattended was pure foolishness. She decided to grab a flashlight and put it in her bag. No one need even know it was there.

Again, she felt foolish for her fears, but there they were. At least with the flashlight, she could get to the lanterns with no issue when she came home.

She went back outside to see another buggy drawing near.

"Why, it's Noah," Martha commented from where she waited by her buggy door.

Had he come for her, too? Leora's heart gave a happy jolt. "Just a minute," she told Martha.

She ran back to Noah's buggy as he drew to a halt. She went to his window. "Hello, Noah."

"I came by to fetch you for the prayer meeting."

Even in the cold, her cheeks warmed with pleasure. "Thank you, but Tom and Martha are here."

He nodded slowly. "I'm too late." He smiled at her. "You going with them, then?"

She hesitated, but only for a minute. It would create much less gossip if she went with Martha and her family. She could only imagine the tongues wagging if she showed up riding beside Noah King.

"*Jah*," she said.

"I'll see you there." He smiled again and snapped his reins, pulling his buggy around Tom's and leaving the drive.

Leora ran back and climbed in the back of Tom's and Martha's buggy, to sit beside their two *kinner*.

"Hello, Louisa and Ben," she said. "How are you two doing?"

They both grinned up at her.

"Someone's burnin' our barns," Ben announced.

Leora's brow raised. Martha had gotten in by then, and she turned to her son. "We're going to pray for them," she said.

"So they don't burn 'em no more," Ben said, tugging at Leora's cape.

"*Jah*, Ben. We're going to pray so the fires stop." Leora looked at Martha, who was giving her a frank look.

"Well?" Martha said.

"Well, what?"

"Why did Noah come by?"

Leora bit her lip before answering. "Um. He was going to give me a ride to the prayer meeting."

"I see." Martha's expression turned playful. "And here Tom and I ruined your plans."

"We didn't have plans," Leora was quick to say.

"Hmm. So, he's been coming over frequently, huh?"

"I never said that."

Martha laughed and nudged Tom. "Noah is sweet on our Leora," she said.

"*Nee!* He isn't," Leora insisted.

Martha reached back and tickled Ben, who giggled. "Did you hear that, Ben? Noah is sweet on Leora."

"Martha," Leora cried. "Ben will get ideas and tell everyone!"

"*Nee,* he won't." She looked seriously at Ben. "It'll be our secret, won't it?"

Ben's eyes grew wide, and he nodded solemnly. "Our secret," he repeated.

"But seriously, Leora. What's going on?"

Leora glanced at Tom who didn't seem to be listening. But then, how could he not? She gave Martha a pleading look.

Martha snorted. "*Ach,* don't mind Tom. He's deaf to this kind of talk, *ain't so*, Tom?"

"Completely deaf," Tom responded, deadpan.

Leora rolled her eyes. How she loved these people. They could always make her laugh. Her tortuous afternoon was forgotten.

"Well, Tom doesn't seem so deaf to me," Leora said, laughing.

"In truth, Noah has been giving me rides to work sometimes. And he took me to Marlie's after the fire."

"I heard you spent the night," Martha said.

"Along with Noah," Tom interjected.

Martha's mouth dropped open. "What? How in the world did I miss that little tidbit? *Ach,* Leora. You haven't been telling me a thing."

"We did spend the night in her front room," Leora said. Then she grew serious. "Marlie was shook up. So were the *kinner.* I didn't think she should be alone, and when Noah learned I was staying, he stayed, too. I suppose he thought we should have a man around."

"I think he was right," Tom said. "I'm glad he stayed. Marlie caught sight of who probably set the fire."

Martha gasped. "What? I didn't hear that either. Goodness, what's happening with me? I'm missing all the news."

"She saw someone with a hood on," Leora told her. "She thinks it was the person who set the fire."

"*Ach,*" Martha murmured.

Leora chose not to share about her shed incident. She wasn't sure why she kept it to herself. Maybe by not talking about it, it became less real. But whatever the reason, she kept quiet.

"We're here," Tom announced.

"Now, *kinner*," Martha said, "you're to be on your best behavior. This is the bishop's house we're at. Do you understand?"

Ben nodded, and Louisa just stuck her fingers in her mouth. There were already a good number of buggies in the yard, lined up in a tidy row. The horses were still hitched up, though, so Leora assumed the prayer meeting wouldn't be too long. They climbed out of the buggy and filed into the already crowded house.

"Welcome," said the bishop's wife. "It's right crowded in here, but the barn is so cold today."

"We don't mind," Martha said kindly, shepherding her children to where the women were gathered. Tom disappeared into the men.

Leora couldn't help but look for Noah. He was in the back, but he was tall enough to be seen. He caught her eye and smiled. She turned away quickly, embarrassed to be noticed looking for him.

After about ten minutes, the bishop spoke.

"Thank you for coming," he said. "As you all know, we've been targeted by someone. We don't know their reasons for attacking us, but it's not the first time."

"First time for us in Hollybrook," someone behind Leora murmured.

"We're here to pray for them—whoever they are. And for our own strength and patience and love. We know that meeting violence with violence is never the answer."

He went on for another five minutes or so before they began to pray. It was a silent prayer, and Leora felt a peace fill her. She loved to be in the middle of her community when they were praying. Even the occasional sniffle or whine from a child didn't interrupt the calm feeling of love and faith and hope. She wasn't sure how long their praying lasted; she only knew when the bishop cleared his throat to signify the end of the prayer time, she felt better than she had for days.

Everyone else must have felt the same, for the heavy feeling at the beginning of the meeting had been transformed to one of lightness and joy at being together. The chatting started and then the laughter. The children crawled down from their mothers' laps and began running around, darting between people's legs.

Noah made his way over to her. "Is everything all right at your place, Leora? Nothing else happen?"

She glanced around, but no one seemed to have heard his words.

"Everything is fine," she told him.

"You staying with Martha tonight?"

She shook her head. "There's no need."

He looked disgruntled for a moment, but then he smiled. "Do you need a ride into the diner tomorrow?"

"I'm planning to go in about ten o'clock."

"I'll be there to take you," he said, and before she could respond, he moved away, joining the men who appeared to be busy planning the barn raisings.

Martha stepped close and whispered, "You like him, Leora. Admit it."

Leora lowered her voice to a murmur. "Of course, I like him. Everyone does. He's a nice man."

Martha laughed outright at that. "*Jah*, Leora. That's what I meant." She nudged Leora and shook her head in amusement.

Leora's cheeks flamed hot. "Someone's going to hear you."

Martha laughed again. "*Ach,* no one's paying us a bit of mind."

Leora fidgeted with her *kapp* strings and unable to help herself, her gaze went to Noah. He cut a fine figure, there, in the middle of the men. His shoulders were broad, and his shirt strained the slightest bit over his muscles. She found herself wondering what it would be like to be enveloped in his embrace every morning and evening.

She gave a start and blinked hard. She looked back to Martha who was giving her a knowing look.

"Like I said..." Martha whispered, one eyebrow raised.

Leora scowled. "Fine," she said. "I suppose I'm the tiniest bit smitten."

Martha's face broke out into a wide smile. "*Ach*, Leora, but that's *gut*. He's a fine man."

"I said the tiniest bit!"

Martha gave that knowing look again, and Leora wanted to fall through the floor. She loved Martha dearly, but sometimes she was completely annoying.

"You're still planning on coming for Thanksgiving, *ain't so?*" Martha asked.

"*Jah*. I'll come over early and help with all the cooking."

"*Mamm* will be there early, too, so we'll get things done in plenty of time." Martha rubbed her protruding stomach. "I'm glad I had the foresight to invite Noah to dinner."

Leora was pleased to hear about the invitation, but considering their conversation, she wasn't about to say so.

"I will bring squash pies," Leora offered.

"Would you? That'd be right nice." Martha let out a small moan. "I don't know why, but this *boppli* I'm carrying sure does kick a lot."

Leora felt a quick flash of envy for her friend. Again, she felt the yearning to have a little one of her own. Her eyes flicked to Noah again. He looked over and their gazes locked. Leora sucked in a breath and averted her eyes. *Can he tell?* she wondered. *Can he tell that I'm growing fond of him?*

Would he ask again to take her driving? Not to any destination, but just to court her? Why had she been so quick to stay silent with him the last time? Right then, she couldn't imagine ever turning Noah down. Her brow furrowed. She had lied to Martha. This was much more than the slightest bit smitten. Why, she was falling in love with the man.

David... What would David think of him? What would he think of her?

Ben tugged on her dress. She bent down close. "Hello, Ben. What do you want?"

"I'm thirsty."

Martha heard him, too. "I'll give you a drink when we get home. Quit bothering Leora."

"It's no bother," Leora told her. "Come on, Ben. I'm sure the bishop's wife has a drink of water for you."

She took Ben's pudgy little hand in her own, and they went to find a glass of water.

Chapter Nineteen

The meeting broke up and Tom and Martha took Leora home and let her off at her house.

"You all right by yourself?" Tom asked.

"Of course, I am. Thanks for the ride."

"Come over soon, and we'll talk more about Thanksgiving," Martha told her.

"Sounds fine," Leora said, climbing out of the buggy. She went inside hurriedly, only glancing swiftly at her shed before going into the dark house. She locked the door and took out her flashlight, shining the beam directly at the table where she'd left her lantern. She got it lit and then put the flashlight away.

She stoked the fire, and it wasn't long before the front room warmed up nicely. She should eat something, but she found she wasn't hungry. Instead, she sank into her rocker next to the warming stove and closed her eyes. After the fellowship of the prayer meeting, she found herself feeling lonely.

Odd, but she usually didn't feel lonely. Oh, of course, she missed David, but that had faded into a dull ache that came intermittently. At first after he'd died, the aching had consumed her. But now, most of the time, she was happy enough. She had her house, she had her work, and she'd managed to whittle down their debt to almost nothing.

Her needs were met, and for that she was grateful.

Yet more and more of late, she felt lonely. More and more of late, she wanted a child. Someone to hold in her arms, to care for, to nurture.

When she'd gone to work at the diner, it had helped. Donna was a nice person, and she was pleasant to be around. And then, there was Bill. He was so attentive, and it was like a salve on her spirit. He made her feel better... She'd tried to keep her wits about her where he was concerned, for she knew a relationship—any kind of relationship—with him could go nowhere. But she liked him, and she had to confess that she liked the attention he gave her.

Now Noah had come more and more into the picture. She'd never really considered him as a beau, but now she could hardly think of anything else. She knew he liked her; he'd made that clear.

"Ask me again," she whispered into the warming air. "Ask me to go riding again, Noah."

She pushed her feet gently on the floor, rocking softly.

"Ask me again," she repeated.

Just then, she heard a banging noise. She shot up out of her chair, her eyes wide. What was that? It sounded like her shed door. Had the wind come up? She ran to the window and peered outside toward the row of evergreen bushes on the far side of her house. In the moonlight, she could see them swaying and bobbing. So, there was a wind. She needed to go outside and secure the latch on the shed.

Her throat went dry. *Was he back? The hooded man? Was he back?*

Because she now had no doubt that it was him who had been there earlier. Was he setting her shed on fire? She tried to swallow, but her throat was now so dry it felt like chalk.

She ran for her flashlight and turned it on.

Go out there. Go out there. Go out there, she told herself.

Her hands were shaking so badly, she could barely fasten her cape. No. She should stay inside. Who cared if the shed door banged all night? But what if it was on fire? She raced to the kitchen, and dousing the flashlight, she pressed her face to the glass of the window. She craned her neck farther than ever, and she could barely make out the shed. And yes, the door was hanging open, moving slightly back and forth.

Maybe, in her nervousness earlier, she hadn't made sure the latch was secure.

She would go out there. She wasn't afraid. She was brave. She had insisted on staying there alone that night, so she was brave.

Wasn't she?

Her thoughts in a whirl, she forced herself to go out the side door, but this time, she was careful to lock it behind her. She drew in a cold breath and flipped on her flashlight. The light bobbed over the hard ground as she made her way to the shed. When she neared, she saw the shed door inch its way closed. It ... wasn't ... the ... wind...

She ran to the shed and slammed it completely closed, securing the latch with trembling fingers. Before she could turn and race back inside, a buggy started down her drive. She gaped at it open-mouthed. She couldn't move. It was as if her feet were frozen to the ground. And then she recognized Flicker, and she went flying over the ground to meet the buggy.

Noah jumped out and she threw herself in his arms. He held her close, his mouth near her ear.

"There, there," he crooned. "What is it? What's happened. There, there..."

She held on for dear life, nearly crushing Noah in her embrace. She didn't budge from his arms until she realized what she was doing. Then she pushed away from his chest, totally embarrassed.

"*Ach,* I'm sorry," she muttered.

He leaned close to her face. "I saw your flashlight..."

She blinked. How? Had he just been passing by? And how strange that he would be passing at that very moment...

"How?" she asked. "How did you see me?"

He cleared his throat as if embarrassed. "I-I was worried about you. I decided to sleep in my buggy across the road from your house."

She stared into his shadowed face. "What?" she whispered.

"I was worried. Don't be angry with me."

Angry? How could she be angry? She was so overcome with relief and gratitude, she couldn't speak.

"Why were you outside, Leora? What were you doing?"

And then she snapped back to the moment. "There's... I think he's in my shed again. It's ... it's him. I just *know* it."

Noah went stiff. "Again?" He took the flashlight from her hand and stepped around her. When she moved with him, he stopped.

"Go inside," he told her. "Go inside, and I'll check it out."

"*Nee,*" she pleaded. "I'll check with you."

"Leora, please. I want you safe."

"I'll walk behind you," she promised. "I'll stay behind you."

He tucked her behind him with his left arm, and she inched forward so close to him that her face grazed the back of his woolen coat.

He unlatched the shed and pulled open the door. Something rushed at them, shoving hard. In the flurry, Noah nearly toppled back onto Leora.

"Stop!" he yelled.

The hooded person darted away and flew across the yard, Noah in pursuit, the beam of the flashlight jerking wildly across the ground as Noah ran. Leora clasped her hand to her chest.

"Noah!" she screamed. "Noah!"

The moon was out, so she wasn't in complete darkness. Panic gripped her, and she didn't know what to do. Her heart pounded wildly in her chest.

"Noah!" she cried again.

But she couldn't see anything now. Not his shadow running. Not the flashlight. Not the hooded man.

She was shaking. What should she do?

She ran to her house and fumbled in the dark to get the door unlocked. She hurried inside the house and snatched up the lantern with a shaking hand. She raced back outside and made her way as fast as she could across her yard and onto the street. The phone shanty wasn't too far away. She only had to reach that. She would get help. It wasn't far... She increased her speed, doing her best not to stumble on the road. She heart hammered inside her, and she listened with all her might and still didn't hear anything.

Noah, be safe, be safe, be safe, she chanted as she neared the phone shanty. She picked her way through the dry weeds and opened the shanty door. Once inside, she reached for the phone with a trembling hand and dialed 9-1-1.

The cold air bit at Noah's face as he kept running. In front of him, he could barely see the shadow of the hooded man. Then he saw him more clearly. He was darting into an empty field. *Dumb,* Noah thought. He could see him better now. See clearly where he was going. Noah's long legs stretched out as he gained speed and closed in on the runner ahead of him.

He could hear the guy panting now; he was slowing down, his sweatshirt flapping behind him.

"Stop!" Noah cried between gasps. "Stop!"

Of course, the man didn't stop. Noah increased his speed until he thought his lungs would explode, but he kept on. He had to. This man *had to be stopped.*

With an agonizing yelp, the man tripped and fell headlong onto the frozen dirt. Within seconds, Noah was on him. He pinned him down, and the hooded guy was no match for Noah's strength. Noah was panting heavily, and he felt heady, as if he were about to pass out, but he kept his grip tight.

"I won't hurt you," Noah rasped out between gulping breaths. "But you ain't going anywhere."

The man fought him, cursing and squirming wildly. Noah held on for dear life.

In the distance, he heard sirens. Had Leora called the police? *Gut girl,* he thought. But how would the police know where they were? And then Noah saw the flashlight lying on the ground at a crazy angle where he'd flung it, shining its light into the sky.

The man beneath him continued to struggle, but he was so much thinner, so much lighter than Noah, he didn't stand a chance. The police car came to a grinding halt in the gravel at the side of the road.

"Over here!" Noah called.

Within seconds, the police were there, and Noah loosened his grip.

One of the policemen shone his light in the guy's face. "Oh Lord. It's you," he said. "Read him his rights, Gerry."

The other policeman recited his spiel while the first one

cuffed the man. Noah wiped the sweat from his face and looked at the guy more closely. He was just a kid. Couldn't be more than sixteen or seventeen years old.

"Playing with matches again?" the first policeman asked. He glanced at Noah. "You all right?"

"I'm fine."

"Thanks for your good work tonight."

Noah nodded and just then, he saw lantern light bobbing down the road. *Leora.* It had to be her.

"How'd you catch him?" the policeman called Gerry asked Noah.

"He was in Leora Fisher's shed. I don't know why. He didn't set it on fire."

The face of the kid was something to behold. Noah didn't remember ever seeing such hatred on anyone's face, adult or teen. Was the hatred directed at him? Or at all the Amish?

"His parents reported him missing two weeks ago. I imagine he was seeking shelter wherever he could find it..." Gerry said.

"But the fires..."

"It's not his first rodeo," the first policeman said. "He served time in juvie for setting fires two years ago. Come on, son. We're taking you in."

Noah stood there, watching, as they dragged the boy, kicking and cursing across the field. Noah was still panting, and his heart was still racing.

"Noah?" called Leora from the edge of the field.

"I'm coming, Leora," he called back.

The first policeman turned back to him. "We may need to ask you more questions. Your name?"

"Noah King."

"All right. Good night, Mr. King."

"*Gut* night."

Leora was picking her way over the dirt, her lantern swathing her in a sheath of yellow light.

"Are you all right, Noah?"

"I'm fine." He snatched up the flashlight and went to join her.

"I called the police…"

He cupped her cheek. "Thank you," he murmured. "It's over now."

Leora's eyes were filled with tears. Any moment, they would fall.

"I'll take you back home," he said, his voice thick with emotion. With God's grace, there would be no more fires now. No more lost barns.

"Was... Was he the one who did it? The fires?" Leora asked quietly.

Noah nodded. "They think so. He's set them before. The police knew him."

She was silent as they turned toward her home.

"He's just a kid, Leora. A kid."

"Is he?"

"*Jah*. No more than seventeen I'd guess."

She drew in a breath.

He shook his head. "Imagine doing something that hateful at such a young age."

"He must be very troubled."

"He must be."

They fell into step on the road, walking slowly, both their lights going before them and illuminating the asphalt.

"Noah?"

"Hmm?"

"You were going to spend the night in your buggy?"

He looked down at her. Her eyes were wide, and her expression was one of both awe and gratitude.

"I was," he said tenderly.

She visibly swallowed. "Thank you." Her voice was a whisper, but it carried with it such a sense of intimacy that his heart swelled.

"Leora?"

She bit the edge of her lip before answering. "*Jah?*"

"Will you go riding with me some evening?"

This time, she didn't hesitate. "I will," she said. She smiled then, and to him, it seemed like the darkness around them receded into pure light.

He grabbed her free hand, and they continued walking toward her home.

Chapter Twenty

The day before Thanksgiving, Leora worked on a huge batch of fresh rolls for the meal. She'd decided earlier that bringing only squash pies wasn't enough of a contribution, so she'd told Martha she'd also bring the rolls. They had risen perfectly and were now in the oven. She was busy rolling out dough for the pie crusts.

She'd already baked the squash and mashed it, mixing it with spices and milk. It smelled delicious, and she hoped it tasted the same. Ever since the other night when Noah had caught the arsonist, Leora couldn't stop smiling. Her fear of being alone had evaporated as soon as the police had left with the young man in cuffs.

But that really wasn't her reason for smiling.

Noah King. He was her reason. *Noah King. Noah King.* She

loved the way his name tumbled off her tongue. She set down her rolling pin and sighed. Goodness, but she was acting like a smitten schoolgirl. She laughed.

Be that as it may, she couldn't have stopped her smiles if she wanted to. She tossed a bit more flour onto the counter and continued her rolling. She still couldn't get over the fact that Noah had planned to stay in his buggy the whole night and watch her house. He'd even brought a blanket for Flicker.

He was a kind man. A good man. Someone who would be a wonderful husband and a wonderful father. She balked.

"Getting a bit ahead of yourself, aren't you?" she whispered.

But was she? The look of love in Noah's eyes that night... It had taken her breath.

"David?" she said aloud. "I-I... Well, I hope you are all right regarding Noah. I know it hasn't been that long since I lost you. I never intended to fall in love again. Truly, I didn't. It just happened. And Noah, well, you know Noah. And you liked him. I do remember that. You are happy for me, aren't you?"

Tears gathered in her eyes and she wiped at them with her forearm, trying not to smear flour on her face. She sniffed. "I still miss you, David. I always will..."

And she would.

His passing had left a huge hole in her heart. The past year had been difficult. Not only because she missed her husband, but because of the mess of debt he'd left her in. That, she wouldn't miss. Her mind wandered. Would Noah ever lead them into such a financial mess?

She didn't think so. But then, she hadn't thought so of David either.

A sudden apprehension gripped her. Maybe she should slow this courtship down. Maybe she should be a lot more careful this time. She simply couldn't bear to go through all of this again.

Her smile faded, and a line of worry creased her brow.

"Noah?" she spoke into the air. "You wouldn't double mortgage your place, would you?"

Maybe Noah owned his farm outright. Maybe he was more careful with his funds. Maybe that horrible year of crops a few years back hadn't devastated him, like it had David.

Maybe...

She huffed out her breath. "Maybe, you should concentrate on your baking," she scolded.

She laid the first crust into the pie plate and started in on the next one.

Later that afternoon, Leora went in to work. She rode her bicycle as there was an unexpected break from the freezing temperatures. Typical for Indiana, everyone said. "Forty degree changes in weather at the drop of a hat."

"Leora Fisher!" Donna chastised her when she saw her. "Don't think I didn't notice that you rode in on your bike. My brother isn't going to be pleased."

"It's at least fifty degrees out there," Leora told her, peeling off her cape. "It's like summer."

Donna snorted. "Hardly."

Leora laughed. "Well, after the cold we've had, it feels like it."

"Leora?" Bill said, coming to the doorway of the kitchen. "You're here. I was about to go and get you in my truck."

"And now you don't need to."

He smiled at her, his eyes twinkling. "No, I don't. You're here —even though I know you don't plan to stay long today."

She squirmed a bit at the obvious pleasure in his voice at seeing her. The image of Noah's face filled her mind. She was going to have to say something to Bill. Or hint at it, anyway. She couldn't have him pining after her.

Shame filled her. She shouldn't have ever let him give her a ride in his truck. Hadn't that been the start of it?

Bill followed her into her small office.

"I wanted to talk to you," he said.

She cringed, dreading what might come next. "*Jah?*"

"I know you have no family around," he started, "and we're open tomorrow on Thanksgiving Day like I told you. But afterward, I mean after the crowds leave, Donna and I are going to enjoy a private Thanksgiving dinner. It'll be really nice. I would love it if you would join us."

She looked at his hopeful face and swallowed hard.

"Please say yes," he continued. "And I'll give you a ride here and back home because it will be dark by then. See..." He grinned widely. "It's all arranged."

"But—" she started.

"I won't take no for an answer."

"I'm spending Thanksgiving Day with Martha and her family."
Tell him, tell him about Noah.

"You could still come. Our meal will be quite late."

"I—"

"Come on, Leora. You know you want to," he teased.

"It's just that... Well, I don't think I should. Noah will likely take me home from Martha's, and he might stay and visit a bit." There. She'd gotten that out, anyway.

Bill's animation faded. "I ... see."

"But thank you so much for the invitation," she added quickly.

He stared at her, his eyes full of questions. "Am I to assume..." He stopped and cleared his throat. "Are you dating Noah now?"

She sucked in a breath. "*Jah*," she murmured. "*Jah*, I am."

Bill blinked rapidly, and she saw a myriad of emotions flicker over his face. "I see," he said again. Then he put on a smile. "Well, that's nice."

And he turned and left her office—just like that. She stood there, staring at the spot where he'd been. And then she sank down into her chair. She'd been right. He was sweet on her. But surely, he had known it could never have worked out between them. Surely, he knew that.

But no. She wasn't at all sure he knew.

The only thing she was sure of was that she'd done the right thing. Bill Jeffreys was a wonderful person. She did like him. But he didn't make her heart sing. Not like Noah did. She pressed her hands to her chest. Yes, she'd done the right thing, but it hadn't made it any easier.

Chapter Twenty-One

Thanksgiving Day dawned with the sun shining brightly over the frozen ground. It was cold again. Leora's breath blew out in steamy puffs when she went out to feed her chickens. She made quick work of her chores and ran back inside. Tom was scheduled to pick her up in less than half an hour. She wanted to be there early so she could help Martha and her mother and sisters with the rest of the preparations.

She didn't bother taking her cape off. She had already packed up the rolls and the pies, ready to take. She banked her fire, knowing it would likely be completely out by the time she returned. Before, she had been quite excited about this meal, but now she felt some reservation. It was her own fault, of course. She'd allowed her mind to loop around the worry of how Noah handled his finances. No matter how much she scolded herself for it, she couldn't seem to stop the cycle, and she was paying the price.

Instead of looking forward to seeing Noah that day, she dreaded it. Honestly, she was disgusted with herself.

She heard Tom's buggy crunching over her gravel drive. She waited a moment and then opened the door. He'd brought Ben with him. Ben tumbled out of the buggy, grinning.

"We're having a big, big, BIG dinner!" he hollered to her.

Leora laughed. "I know we are. It's Thanksgiving."

"*Jah*, it's Thanksgibbing!"

"The food's inside, Tom. I'll help you."

"*Nee*, I'll get it. You go on and get into the buggy with Ben. It's mighty cold again today."

She almost told him to be sure and lock the door, but she forced herself not to. She didn't want to live that way. She supposed some might call her foolish, but there had never been a reason to lock up in Hollybrook before, and she didn't want to make it a habit.

But Tom must have had different ideas. As he was coming out with the first load of food, he asked, "Do you have your key, Leora? I'll lock your door for you when I go back for the pies."

She opened her mouth to protest, but then realized Martha

would likely have a fit if she didn't go along with him—even though the arsonist had been safely apprehended.

"*Nee.* I don't have my key. It's hanging right inside the door."

"All right. I'll fetch it and lock up for you."

A few minutes later, he came back out with the last load of food. "Okay. I think I've got everything, and your door is now locked."

After putting the pies on the back seat of the buggy, he handed her the key, and she tucked it into her bag. She nodded her thanks and realized that Noah would be upset right along with Martha, if she didn't have her doors locked.

Noah.

She didn't want to see him—except, she did. *Ach,* but she was driving herself crazy. Thank goodness, Ben chattered all the way to Martha's. He went on and on about the big turkey they were going to eat, and the cookie he'd already eaten. Listening to his jabber lightened Leora's spirits.

"Here we are," Tom declared as they pulled into his drive.

Leora could already see a row of buggies near the barn. It looked like most of Martha's family had already arrived.

"Go ahead in," Tom told her. "I'll bring in the food."

"I can take the rolls," she said. "Come on, Ben. Let's go inside."

She picked up the large basket that held her rolls, and they hurried inside. The minute they passed the door, a wave of delicious heat enveloped them, and the aroma of turkey and spices filled the air. Chatter spilled out from the kitchen, and Leora noticed the men had congregated in the front room. She nodded and smiled her greeting to them and then went on into the kitchen.

"*Ach!* You're here," Martha cried, dropping the spoon she was holding. She held out her hands for the basket of rolls and peered inside. "They look lovely, Leora."

"I hope so."

Tom dropped off the pies before disappearing to join the men.

The women were bustling between the cook stove, the counter, and the table, which was already laden with food. Leora knew the women in Martha's family quite well, and they all greeted her with big smiles. Within seconds, she was peeling potatoes.

"We need to get that platter of pickles and olives put together, too," Martha's mother said.

"I'm doing that," Martha's sister Rose commented.

Leora relaxed immediately. She loved these people, and she was so grateful to be included in their day. The talk moved from what needed doing, to the weather, to the coming Christmas season, to the fires.

It was then that Leora realized Noah was a hero.

"You were there, Leora," Martha's mother said. "Did you see Noah capture that person who started the fires?"

Leora recounted the night.

"So brave..." Martha said. "And notice it happened right after prayer meeting."

"The *gut* Lord heard our cries," Rose said, nodding. "And he provided Noah for us."

"We must continue to pray for that young man," Martha said. She took in a huge breath and rubbed her swollen belly. "I need to sit down."

"Sit," Leora said quickly, pulling out the kitchen bench. "There are plenty of hands here to do the work. You can supervise."

Martha laughed. "Right. Like that will work."

Martha's mother chuckled. "It'll work. We can handle this."

"We can," said Tammy, Martha's other sister.

And they did. No one would let Martha up from the bench the entire morning. She complained a bit but seemed to enjoy her inactivity. Although, little Louisa demanded her attention more than once—until Martha's mother swooped her up and took her in to the men.

It was just before noon when Noah's buggy pulled into the

drive. Leora, who had been listening for it, was the first to notice.

"Noah's here," she announced.

"Why don't you go greet him?" Martha asked, giving her a knowing glance. "Welcome him to the meal."

Letting Noah in was completely unnecessary as he would just come in on his own, but Leora didn't argue with Martha. She wasn't about to have that be a topic of public discussion. She hurriedly wiped her hands on the kitchen towel and went to the front door. She stepped outside without her cape, despite the cold.

Noah had parked the buggy in the row with the others and was unhitching Flicker.

"Leora!" he called to her. "It's *gut* to see you."

She heard the pleasure in his voice, and for a moment she forgot her concerns. "It's *gut* to see you, too."

Just as quickly, though, her concerns came back, hovering over her, poking at her mind. She did her best to squash them, wanting to enjoy this special day.

But Noah was entirely too observant for that. "What is it?" he asked, pausing what he was doing. "What's happened?"

She frowned. "Nothing. Everything is fine."

"*Nee*," he said, studying her face. "Something is bothering you."

She let out her breath in exasperation. He was entirely too sensitive to her moods.

"You can tell me, Leora," he said softly, stepping closer. "You can tell me anything."

But how in the world could she tell him that she was afraid? That she was worried he was as careless with money as her David had been?

"Leora?"

"Are you in debt?" she blurted, and then horrified, she clapped her hand over her mouth.

His brow rose. "In debt?"

She didn't answer. She just stared at him wide-eyed, her hand still covering her mouth.

He smiled. "What gave you that idea?"

She dropped her hand. "I... I..." She swallowed hard. "I was just wondering."

He leaned down until his face was close to hers. The steam from his breath fluttered over her skin. "*Nee,* Leora. I'm not in debt. Are you worried about that?"

She took a huge, gulping breath of relief. "I-I'm sorry," she mumbled.

"Why? You can ask me anything, just like I said."

"But... But men don't like—"

He grabbed her hands. "Leora," he said firmly. "Anything. You can ask me anything."

She felt tears welling in her eyes.

"Besides," he went on, "aren't you the genius with finances? That's your job, right? I'd be a fool not to take advantage of you." He laughed. "You know what I mean."

"You'd let me help you with your personal finances?"

"Why wouldn't I?" His face flushed. "I mean, well, if things between us progress."

She shook her head in wonder. David never ever let her do a thing with their finances. He'd told her it was a man's work.

"You're not teasing me?"

Noah frowned. "Where is this coming from? Don't you trust me? I would welcome your help if we were a couple. And I'd expect you to welcome mine." The lines of concern on his forehead disappeared. He laughed again. "Of course, I can't cook worth a bean."

She began to laugh. "Well, don't you worry about that. I can."

Their gazes locked, and something passed between them. An understanding. A glimpse into the future. A promise of what was to come.

"Can I help you unhitch Flicker?" she asked.

"Why not? We'll do it together," he said, smiling. "It's Thanksgiving Day, Leora. Isn't that wonderful *gut?*"

"It is, indeed," she responded.

And it was wonderful good. Leora helped Noah put Flicker into the barn with the other horses, and then she slipped her hand around his elbow. Together, they walked toward the warm house that was filled to the brim with dear friends and the scent of a wonderful feast to come.

The End

Continue Reading...

✿

Thank you for reading **Thanksgiving in Hollybrook! Are you wondering what to read next?** Why not read **The Twin?** **Here's a peek for you:**

"It's not fair," Rachel hissed. "It should be me."

"Why?" Lindy asked. "There's no real reason."

Rachel drew herself up and glared at her older sister. "*Jah*, there is a reason, and you know it."

Lindy sighed. She was weary of Rachel, weary of her constant complaints and whining. It wasn't Lindy's fault that *Dat* had chosen her for the job—despite what Rachel believed.

"You get to see him every day. And *all* day." Rachel walked to the door of Lindy's bedroom and huffed. "It should be me."

"I'm not there for Robert Mast, as you're well aware. I'm there to care for his mother." Lindy frowned, remembering Berta Mast's pain the day before. Lindy had done her best to ease it, using all sorts of concoctions Old Mae had put together for her, but Lindy knew they hadn't helped much.

Rachel's brow crinkled. "How is she?"

"Not *gut*."

"Yesterday was a bad day?"

"A very bad day." Lindy took a fresh *kapp* from her top drawer and bobby-pinned it in place. "I hope today is better."

"So do I." Rachel drew in a long breath. "Sorry, Lindy. I shouldn't be fussing so."

"*Nee*, you shouldn't," Lindy answered frankly. "I didn't ask for this job, and I certainly didn't connive to take it from you."

"I know," Rachel said quickly. "I know."

"*Dat* doesn't even know you're sweet on Robert."

"Or that you're sweet on Reuben," Rachel added.

It was ironic that they as sisters, had fallen for brothers. Robert and Reuben were identical twins, so identical in fact, that it was difficult to tell them apart. Lindy didn't dare mention that sometimes when she was with Robert, she felt as though she were with Reuben instead. Rachel would have a fit if she knew...

Yet, Lindy never really forgot that Robert wasn't Reuben. Reuben was gone, and she missed him. It seemed like years since he'd left for Ohio to help his cousin with planting and harvest—years instead of just months.

The longest months of Lindy's life.

"Tell Robert hello for me," Rachel said.

"Of course, I will." Lindy moved to the door, and Rachel stepped aside to let her pass. "I need to be going. I thought to stop at the Feed & Supply on the way to get some more honey. Berta likes it in her tea."

VISIT HERE To Read More:

http://ticahousepublishing.com/amish.html

Thank you for Reading

If you **love Amish Romance**, **Visit Here:**

https://amish.subscribemenow.com/

to find out about all **New Hollybrook Amish Romance Releases! We will let you know as soon as they become available!**

If you enjoyed *Thanksgiving in Hollybrook!* would you kindly take a couple minutes to leave a positive review on Amazon? It only takes a moment, and positive reviews truly make a difference. I would be so grateful! Thank you!

Turn the page to discover more Amish Romances just for you!

More Amish Romance for You

We love clean, sweet, rich Amish Romances and have a lovely library of Brenda Maxfield titles just for you! (Remember that ALL of Brenda's Amish titles can be downloaded FREE with Kindle Unlimited!)

If you love bargains, you may want to start right here!

VISIT HERE to discover our complete list of box sets!

http://ticahousepublishing.com/bargains-amish-box-sets.html

VISIT HERE to find Brenda's single titles:

http://ticahousepublishing.com/amish.html

You're sure to find many favorites. Enjoy!

About the Author

I am blessed to live in part-time in Indiana, a state I share with many Amish communities, and part-time in Costa Rica. One of my favorite activities is exploring other cultures. My husband, Paul, and I have two grown children and five precious grandchildren. I love to hole up in our lake cabin and write. You'll also often find me walking the shores by the sea. Happy Reading !

https://ticahousepublishing.com/